"You got what you wanted all along, and you don't have to sleep with the boss's daughter to keep it!"

"What if I want to?" Jarrod pulled Gena to him. Their faces were very close, and she could feel his breath against her lips. Then his mouth came down on hers in a kiss of fierce desire.

It was just too easy to open her mouth to him, to let him take control again. But too much time had passed, Gena thought bitterly, and pulled away. There was no way she was letting Jarrod Saxon back in her life!

"What's the matter, Jarrod," she asked heatedly, "are the people back home giving you a hard time, asking awkward questions? *Isn't it strange that Jarrod inherited what should have been Gena's, and now she's nowhere to be found? Do you think he killed her?*"

Jarrod's hand circled her throat, and Gena couldn't repress the thrill that shot through her at his touch. "There's a thought," he said softly. "When I finally found you, after ten long months of thinking I'd never see you again, wondering if you'd found someone else, I couldn't decide whether to kill you or make love to you." He smiled then, and the effect of the smile went straight through her, making her shiver. "But then the anger was conquered by need—the need to have you in my arms again, in my bed . . ."

WHAT ARE *LOVESWEPT* ROMANCES?

They are stories of true romance and touching emotion. We believe
those two very important ingredients are constants in our highly sensual
and very believable stories in the *LOVESWEPT* line. Our goal is to give
you, the reader, stories of consistently high quality that may sometimes
make you laugh, sometimes make you cry, but are always fresh and
creative and contain many delightful surprises within their pages.

Most romance fans read an enormous number of books. Those they
truly love, they keep. Others may be traded with friends and soon
forgotten. We hope that each *LOVESWEPT* romance will be a
treasure—a "keeper." We will always try to publish

LOVE STORIES YOU'LL NEVER FORGET
BY AUTHORS YOU'LL ALWAYS REMEMBER

The Editors

LOVESWEPT® • 181

Fayrene Preston
Robin and Her Merry
People

ROBIN AND HER MERRY PEOPLE
A Bantam Book / February 1987

If you would be interested in receiving protective vinyl
covers for your Loveswept books, please write to this address
for information:

Loveswept
Bantam Books
P.O. Box 985
Hicksville, NY 11802

ISBN 0-553-21790-9

Published simultaneously in the United States and Canada

Bantam Books are published by Bantam Books, Inc. Its trademark, consisting of the words "Bantam Books" and the por-
trayal of a rooster, is Registered in U.S. Patent and Trademark
Office and in other countries. Marca Registrada. Bantam
Books, Inc., 666 Fifth Avenue, New York, New York 10103.

PRINTED IN THE UNITED STATES OF AMERICA

O   0 9 8 7 6 5 4 3 2 1

One

Concealed in the shadowy interior of his car, Jarrod Saxon watched Gena DuMont Alexander stroll down the sidewalk toward him. In some respects it seemed only yesterday that he had last seen her. In other respects it seemed like years. In reality it had been only ten months—ten *long* months—since she had run away from him.

The impact of seeing her again made every muscle in his body coil painfully.

He had hired the services of the best team of detectives money could get, to scour the country for her. And for months they had been unable to turn up anything. He hadn't faulted their skill, though. She had hidden herself well. Finally, the detectives had called to say they had found her.

He could still remember the relief he had felt. And the anger.

The street was in one of the oldest neighborhoods in Dallas, just blocks away from downtown. From his car window the skyline of the city loomed large and bold. Compared to its modern steel and concrete, this street seemed an anachronism.

The architecture of the houses varied, as did their size. Large two-story homes sat next to small bungalows. The houses must have been built in the twenties, Jarrod judged.

Some of the houses, he noticed, had been restored. Two appeared to be in the process of renovation, but most were in need of repair.

He cast a quizzical glance at the old house where the detective report said Gena lived. Who would have thought she'd be living in one small room in such a place? But then again, who ever would have thought that Gena would be earning her living as a waitress?

Inevitably questions sprang to mind, but he told himself they didn't matter. He had found her, and she would be going home with him tonight. That was the most important thing.

Jarrod strained, trying to get a better look at her. Did she seem preoccupied? No. Actually she seemed content, almost peaceful. His mouth tightened. He hadn't drawn a peaceful breath in ten months.

As she drew closer he searched for changes in her. He found nothing obvious, except perhaps her clothes. He was used to seeing her in silk, not denim.

Jeans hugged the long length of her legs. He remembered those same slim legs, naked and wrapped around him, her heels digging into the backs of his thighs, as their bodies surged together.

Today her pale gold hair was pulled back into a braid. He remembered her hair so well. How fine and soft it was, how it shimmered down her back past her waist. And—a fire flickered within the depths of his dark eyes as the thought came to him—how when they made love, the long strands would wind around them, binding them together.

A green T-shirt skimmed over her upper body. He could tell that something was written across it in white letters, but at this distance he couldn't read what it said. From the detective report he knew she worked in a bar called Clancey's. Perhaps, he thought, the shirt was part of her uniform. The idea of Gena DuMont Alexander in a uniform should have been laughable, since she had left behind three closets full of exquisite designer clothes, but Jarrod could find nothing laughable in any of this.

A cream-colored cardigan sweater had been thrown across her shoulders, the sleeves tied so that they fell casually over her breasts. With no effort at all his mind formed a picture of how her breasts had filled his hands, and unconsciously he flexed his fingers.

Damn her anyway! he thought. How dare she run away from him!

A breeze cartwheeled gold and scarlet leaves across the sidewalk and rustled through the branches of the tall, stately live oaks far above Gena's head. A faint fragrance of chrysanthemums came to her in the crisply scented air. An unconscious smile touched her lips as she savored the beauty of the Indian summer day.

Suddenly she grimaced as her foot came down on a sharp rock. The pressure of it through the thin leather of her shoe made her foot throb—not a new sensation lately, she thought dryly.

Since she had gone to work at Clancey's, she had gained the utmost respect for waitresses and anyone else whose job demanded that you remain on your feet for eight or more hours a day while you did your best to make a living. Waitressing was hard, thankless work, and even after ten months her feet had not become accustomed to the abuse. She supposed she could blame her tender feet on the "aristocratic arches" her mother had once proudly claimed that Gena had inherited from her.

Many times Gena had pondered how horrified her mother would be, if she were alive, to know that her carefully brought up daughter was working in a bar-café in Texas!

She strode up the walkway that led to the house and paused to look at the wonderful old place that was now her home. Its brick facade was austere and plain, with a porch that ambled along the front of the house and around one side. Pots of ferns dotted the porch, and a wooden swing hung from one end. She supposed some people would look at the structure and see a house that was shabby and in disrepair. But to her the brick Victorian house presented a solid, comfortable refuge for the people who lived in it.

She skipped up the steps to the porch, opened the glass-paneled door, and crossed the oak floor of the foyer.

Sugar MacIntosh, Gena's landlady, stuck her head out the door of her apartment. "Oh, good, Gena, it's you!"

Despite her throbbing feet, Gena smiled, for Sugar had that kind of effect on people. She had hazel eyes that habitually twinkled, and a square-shaped face that invariably boasted a great deal of rouge and rice powder, a makeup practice left over from her days in the theater.

Many times Gena had tried to judge Sugar's age, but she had always failed. She knew only that her neighbor's much-beloved husband, Tex, had been dead for the past ten years. The still-grieving widow had confided that Tex loved her in toreador pants. Fortunately Sugar's small, neat figure hadn't changed much in ten years, because she still wore the pants faithfully. A special favorite was the pink satin pair she sported at the moment.

"How's your day been?" Sugar asked. "So far, I mean."

"My day's been pretty hectic," Gena said. "The lunch crowd keeps getting bigger and bigger, and Clancey's smile gets wider and wider. For the last few months there hasn't been a day that I haven't tripped over at least one briefcase."

Sugar shook her head, and her hair, approximately the color of cotton candy and sprayed with roughly a can and a half of hair spray, stayed rigidly in place. "All these uptown people coming into the area. It's not like the old days, but then, not much is."

For a moment Gena thought a shadow might have crossed Sugar's usually cheerful face, but in the next instant she decided she was wrong.

"Where's Rose?" Sugar asked, naming another occupant of the house, also a waitress at Clancey's.

"She'll be along soon. She stayed behind to argue with Clancey. He's so taken with his new customers, these so-called young, upwardly mobile professionals, that he's considering all sorts of changes to cater to them. But Rose says one hint of a hanging fern or a little umbrella dangling out of a funny-colored frozen drink, and she's out the door." Gena grinned. "Clancey's really letting these new people go to his head."

Sugar allowed an inelegant snort to escape her delicate nostrils. "You mean, his wallet!" Fingernail polish, the exact pink shade of Sugar's hair, gleamed as she waved one hand in the air. "This whole community is slowly but surely being Yuppi-fied."

Something in Sugar's voice caused Gena to look at her with concern. "I know it must be hard for you to see your old neighborhood change after so many years, Sugar, but it's not entirely a bad thing. The influx of these people is rejuvenating the area. I do agree, though, that Clancey is getting a little carried away. Rose can draw the line at ferns and cute little umbrellas, but I'm stopping short of those less-than-decent costumes Clancey wants his waitresses to wear."

Sugar's eyes brightened with interest. "Oh?"

"You should see them! They could fit into a thimble."

"But you've got a beautiful figure. Why—you could have been a show girl! And I know all about show girls"—Sugar patted her hair—"what with my stage experience."

"Uh, yes." Gena didn't want to get caught in a conversation, the subject of which was Sugar's show-business experience. She knew such discussions could go on for hours. "Listen, can we talk later? My feet have been looking forward to a good soaking."

"Okay, but we really do need to get together and plan our Thanksgiving dinner." This time the shadow that crossed Sugar's face stayed long enough for Gena to be certain of what she was seeing. "So many people are coming, you know."

Was it just the dinner Sugar was worrying about? Gena felt a wave of relief. That was easily solvable! "Thanksgiving is weeks away. We have plenty of time yet, and even if we didn't, there's nothing to worry about." She had acted as her father's hostess innumerable times, at dinners far more complicated than the potluck, neighborhood Thanksgiving get-together she and Sugar were planning.

Sugar looked undecided. "Do you have to work tonight?"

Gena nodded. "I work a split shift today. I go back in at four to get ready for the dinner crowd." She paused. "Sugar, is there something else bothering you?" The older woman's response reassured her.

"Goodness, no! You run along now and rest. Just let me know when's a good time for you—and we'll talk."

"Fine. And really, don't worry about the dinner. Everyone will bring a dish. It'll be easy. You'll see."

The top floor of Sugar's house was divided into four individual apartments—rooms, really, but large ones, with baths attached. One apartment was currently unoccupied, so that for the moment Gena, Rose, and Bertrand were Sugar's only tenants.

Gena took the stairs at a fast pace, eager to get out of her shoes. Maybe she'd even take a little nap, she thought, smiling with anticipation as she unlocked the door of her apartment and went in.

Most of the furniture had been provided by

Sugar. But, finding herself without much money for the first time in her life, Gena had enjoyed using her hands and her imagination to add her own touches. She had wallpapered her room in a soft blue fabric, and used delicate blue print sheets for both the bed and the cushions on the love seat. The iron bed she had painted white, along with the wicker night table, dressing table, and chair.

A small kitchen was hidden behind a folding screen, and the bathroom was only large enough for a claw-footed tub, commode, and white porcelain sink, around which she had gathered a skirt to hide the pipes. The skirt had been stitched out of the same material as the sheet that covered her bed.

She loved her little room. Decorating it had kept her busy during those days just after her arrival in Dallas when she was still struggling with grief over her father's death, and fighting loneliness and the pain of Jarrod's betrayal.

But, she reminded herself firmly, that was something she didn't let herself think about anymore. She had a new life now, complete with friends and a job. If she didn't feel the ecstatic happiness that she had when she and Jarrod were together, she at least had found a certain measure of contentment.

Slipping out of her shoes, she breathed a sigh of relief, then fell back on the bed.

* * *

A knock brought her head up, and Gena looked at the door with mixed feelings. In the nearly ten months she had lived in this house, she had grown to love the other occupants. They had given her just what she needed—unquestioning acceptance—and they had come to depend on her in a thousand little ways. They knew she was always willing to listen to their problems and their daily triumphs and frustrations. But right at this moment, she only wanted to take a nap.

Nevertheless, she shouted, "Come in." The doorknob rattled but stayed securely locked. Drat! With reluctance she pulled herself off the bed and went to answer the door.

But when she opened the door, the smile on her face vanished. Suddenly it felt as though her limbs had hardened into plaster, and she stood as still as a statue. A roaring rose in her ears and a haze of red filled her eyes as her mind struggled in an attempt to reject the fact that Jarrod Saxon was standing before her.

It couldn't be true! And yet . . . She tried to move and couldn't. She attempted to force air into her lungs, but was unable.

Slowly, too slowly, the roaring subsided. Her vision cleared, and she found that he was still standing before her.

"You!" Her mouth formed the word, but she wasn't sure any sound had come out.

Jarrod didn't wait for an invitation, perhaps because he knew one would never be issued. He sauntered into her apartment, calm and deliberate. "Really, Gena, I'm very disappointed in you. Somehow, after ten months I expected something more."

His stance appeared casual, but Gena wasn't fooled. Beneath his calm exterior a storm was brewing.

Panic threatened to choke her, but she had enough presence of mind to know that if she gave way to her emotions, she wouldn't have a chance of coming out of this encounter in one piece. Jarrod was an expert at taking advantage of other people's weaknesses.

Advising herself to take her time, she studied him. He looked the same. Or, on second glance, maybe the angles of his face were more pronounced, harsher. But Gena supposed that was to be expected. After all, he was now head of two corporations, and the energy—and the ruthlessness—such a position required were bound to have taken their toll.

Nothing else had changed, though, she decided. He was still as leanly handsome as ever, with arresting dark brown eyes and equally dark brown hair.

Her gaze skimmed his navy-blue pinstriped suit. During the time she had considered herself in love with Jarrod, she had come to the conclusion that he had a unique way of wearing clothes. It always seemed as though the fabric of the garment had been created expressly to mold and define his tall, muscular frame. There was no denying that there was a definite quality of elegance about Jarrod, but that elegance was underlaid by a strong layer of sensuality. He was a man who would never become lost in a crowd.

Jarrod Saxon.

The man she had loved.

The man who had betrayed her.

The man whom she had secretly betrayed in return.

The man who now had every reason to put her in jail.

Did he know?

She backed away from him, her hands clenching into tight balls at her side. "Get out!"

He tilted his head to one side, as if giving her words serious consideration. "No. That's not it," he said, his voice sarcastic. "I expected something more like, 'I missed you, Jarrod. I'm so glad to see you.'" He shut the door behind him with a definite click, and murmured softly, "Try again, Gena."

"Get out!"

As if she hadn't spoken, his gaze swept the room. What he saw surprised him. He never would have thought Gena would choose to live in this small, cheaply decorated place, with its romantic, Victorian decor. He remembered the luxurious peach-toned suite she had had in her father's home, light-years away from this tiny rented room.

He looked back at her. She was so close, he could feel the heat from her body—and the waves of anger she was exuding. With time, he hoped the anger would fade. As for the heat . . . Lord, but it had been so long. Unable to help himself, he extended a hand to touch her, but with a quick step to the side, she managed to evade him. The muscles along his jaw contracted, and he thrust his hands in his pockets. "Pulling your hair back like that is a crime. Why do you do it?"

"I like it this way," she said, because she sensed he hated it.

His feelings of anger and bewilderment couldn't be contained one second longer. "What in the hell are you doing in this place?"

"Living, and quite happily." Her initial shock at his presence was gone now, although her heart still seemed to be pounding erratically. "How did you find me?"

"Didn't you think I would, Gena? Did you honestly believe that I would let you disappear from my life?" With quick, jerky movements he loosened his tie and undid the top button of his shirt.

"I was hoping you would just forget me."

A smile that held no humor curved his lips. "Then you didn't know me very well."

"That's obvious," she snapped, but immediately regretted her impetuous outburst. It would do no good to lose her temper. "Look, you found me. Congratulations. Now go home!"

"Sure, I'll be glad to." He quickly scanned the room, then strode toward the wardrobe and pulled open the doors.

"Wait! What are you doing? Get away from there."

Jarrod's answer sounded muffled, because he was stooped over, shoving through her clothes. "I'm looking for your suitcase." In a moment he straightened, his hands empty. "Where is it? Under your bed?"

Suddenly she realized that he meant to search the room. "No!" She held up her hand and moved into his path, blocking him. "You can't just come barging in here and go through my things like this! Why would you want my suitcase anyway?"

"We've got seats booked on the six-o'clock flight home."

Six-o'clock flight! She was momentarily stunned by his audacity. *"This* is my home now," she finally said, "and I have no intention of going anywhere with you."

"Gena"—anger had disappeared from his voice, and in its place was a gentle, crooning persuasion—"don't fight me. These last ten months have been hell." His hand went to the side of her neck, and this time she wasn't quick enough to evade him. Brushing one long finger up and down the sensitive skin, he murmured, "We need to talk, babe."

She flinched at the endearment he had used almost exclusively when they had made love. At the same time, though, she could feel her blood heating at his touch. She hated him! she reminded herself.

"Just come home with me," he continued, his

voice flowing over her, the softest of caresses. "I know why you ran, but we can work it out. I can explain."

She jerked away. "I'll just bet you can. I'll bet you've got a whole list of explanations ready. You were always so good with words. You had me right where you wanted me."

In a flash the tone of his voice changed, and each word carried a biting savageness "Evidently I didn't."

Protectively she folded her arms in front of her. "Just for the record, did you know my father was sick?"

"Yes That is . . . I knew he was ill. I just didn't realize it was so serious. No one did. That was the way he wanted it."

She was sorry she had asked. She didn't want to hear his lies. "Get out," she said with quiet firmness. "I ran away because I never wanted to see you again. And in ten months, my feelings haven't changed. If anything, they've gotten stronger." Liar, she silently charged. She had stopped counting the nights she had lain awake, wanting him so badly she was sure the ache in her body would kill her.

Desire and hate. Two powerful emotions that had nearly torn her apart. But she had survived, and she had no intention of having her hard-won peace of mind disturbed now.

He plowed his fingers through his hair, and agitation roughened his voice. "What are you doing here, Gena? You have far too much money to be working as a waitress and living in a one-room apartment!"

"Money! Aren't you forgetting something? It was *you* to whom my father left everything."

"And I told you, I can explain that."

"There's really no need. I was there at the reading of the will. I heard all I needed to."

His eyes darkened. "And then you ran."

"And then I ran." She clenched her hands together. "I've made a new life for myself, Jarrod. I'm happy here."

"You were happy with me once. You can be again."

She gave a light, incredulous laugh. "I don't know why you're so determined to get me back. Is it pride? It that it?"

"I want you back because I love you, dammit!"

His words hurt more than she would have thought possible. "No, Jarrod, you don't. You were in love with my money, but you've got that now. The only reason I can think of that could bring you here is that you're a person who likes everything neatly tied up. I'm a loose end to you. Looking back, I can see that all we had going for us was . . . sexual rapport. Even that would have died between us eventually."

"You're wrong. The fires of our passion grew hotter each time we were together."

He was right about that, she thought miserably. Jarrod had been an expert at many things, and she had been a fast learner. Their lovemaking had taken them inside the gates of heaven. . . .

He saw her flush, and smiled. "You remember, don't you, Gena," he asked softly, "how you used to tremble in my arms? Our bodies would come together as one, and it felt as if we would go up in flames, didn't it? Maybe we both need to remember that feeling again."

Before she knew what he was going to do, he had pulled her into his arms. His mouth came down hard on hers. Gena's body tightened.

She was too calm, he thought. He wanted to force a reaction from her, something that would show him she felt more for him than hate. She still loved him. She had to!

His lips ground into hers. Her taste and scent threatened to overwhelm him. Ten months was a long time! He had no restraint, no control. If he wanted her this desperately, how could she not want him?

She tried to push away from him, but his tongue surged hungrily into her mouth and tangled with hers. Her mind spun as she tried to sort out what was happening. In his kiss there were anger and possessiveness. She remembered his possessive lovemaking and rejected it. She recognized his anger and returned it. Their anger fed their fire. Within her a struggle raged. Never had she been so furious. Never had she needed him more.

With hazy anguish Gena curled her arms around his neck, and her fingers slid through the thickness of his hair.

As the moments went by, their responses began to soften. His hands went to her long braid and unwound it, and he ran his fingers through it until her hair hung shimmering and straight, like a yard of pale gold silk.

His lips journeyed over her face to her ear, and she heard his voice. His husky whisper affected her as much as his kiss. It was the voice with which he had spoken to her during the long, dark nights they had spent together.

"Do you still like this?" he asked as his hand pulled her T-shirt from the waistband of her jeans and caressed her bare back. Though she had tried, she had never forgotten the way his hands could heat her skin, making her go fluid inside.

"And this?" he questioned. He unhooked her bra and brought a hand around to completely cover one of her breasts. Her knees gave way, and she sagged against him.

A growl issued from deep within Jarrod's chest. Damn! Something in his head was telling him that he shouldn't be doing this. He should be trying to explain, to sort things out, but . . . Awkwardly Gena pushed the suit jacket off his shoulders and down his arms. Then, slipping her fingers between the buttons of his shirt, she began to reaquaint herself with the furry warmth of his chest. He dismissed his objections.

"You see, Gena! A passion like ours doesn't die. We never were able to tolerate clothing between us."

As if to prove his point, he slid her T-shirt over

her head, and she damned herself for helping. But her breasts were starved for his touch. And her nipples! The breath caught in her throat as his mouth came down onto one taut peak, and he grasped it carefully between his teeth. It was the first truly gentle gesture he had made since they had started this kiss, and a fresh excitement crashed through her.

Then he was lifting her into his arms, walking the short distance to the bed, and lowering her to the mattress. When he came down on top of her it seemed that her body had eagerly anticipated his weight.

"No one can ever make you feel what I can," he murmured, his mouth at the base of her throat, his tongue tasting the skin over a pounding pulse point. "Distance and time can't change that."

Deliberately he began to move against her, and she felt him, hard and strong against her lower body. As if it were natural, she parted her legs. His pelvis thrust against her, pushing the seam of her jeans into that most sensitive spot, producing an exquisite burst of pleasure.

How could she be letting this happen? Gena asked herself with despair. This was the man who had sweet-talked her father out of her fortune! Help yourself! she ordered.

But, infuriatingly, the tempo of his lovemaking changed; slowed. Jarrod's mouth became coaxing. Shifting his weight, he unsnapped her jeans, and his hand slid beneath them to the silky skin of her abdomen. Just an inch or two more would be all it would take, she thought feverishly as his mouth suckled her breast.

His actions were too erotic to bear with any semblance of sanity. Gena didn't. She arched urgently against him. She wanted him. She needed the release only he could give her.

Jarrod knew her so well. He knew what gave her the most pleasure, knew what could take her to the edge and then over. Damn him! her mind cried while her body pulsated beneath his hands.

She heard herself moan as his caresses crept lower and lower. In just moments his fingers would be in position to . . . Oh, damn! He was right about one thing. He had always been able to transform her into putty, and he still could.

Curiously, it was the expectation of this most intimate act that threw a block up in her mind. If she allowed this lovemaking to continue, it would be an open invitation for Jarrod to reenter her life. And that she couldn't have. Not again!

And there was something else. She had suddenly realized that, except for his jacket, Jarrod was completely dressed. Gena herself was half undressed. To her pleasure-fogged mind, this fact symbolized their entire relationship. She was uncovered, vulnerable. Jarrod was protected, guarded.

Frantically she shoved against him, her breath coming in erratic gasps. "Get up, Jarrod. Get off me!"

"No, babe, no. It's been so long; I've wanted you so badly."

"You can't tell me there haven't been other

women," she charged, attempting to give her anger strength. Where had all her wrath gone? she asked herself. One touch and it had fled like dandelion puffs on a spring wind.

Surprisingly, he stilled; then, after a moment, rolled off her. "Have there been other men, Gena?" he asked quietly. When she didn't answer immediately, he persisted. "There must have been. You're a beautiful, desirable woman, and you've been exposed to men daily in your work."

"Is that all you think it takes?" she asked, her anger flaring. "Being *exposed*, as you put it? You don't know me at all, do you?"

"I put that badly. I'm sorry. But I must know. Are you telling me that you haven't been with other men?"

"I'm not telling you anything, Jarrod." She slid off the bed and reached for her T-shirt. In such a hurry to cover herself, she forgot her bra. Finding it on the floor where Jarrod had so carelessly dropped it, she scooped it up and pushed it into a drawer. She wanted no reminder of how easily she had given in to him. . . . Nearly.

Unfortunately, though, there remained one reminder of her near-indiscretion. The most potent reminder of all: Jarrod, reclining on her bed, looking as if he had every intention of staying there for a long, long time.

Casually, easily, he rearranged his long frame so he was reclining against the pillows. "We're not through, you know."

Gena found his jacket and threw it at him. "We

were through the day the lawyer read Dad's will."
She walked to her dressing table, picked up her
brush, and began thrusting it through her hair.
"Accept it."

"Not a chance."

Her brush strokes became more vigorous. "I
don't understand. You've got what you want,
Jarrod." Again she asked herself, Did he know?
Was this just his way of playing cat and mouse
with her? His response startled her.

"That's exactly right." He slid off the bed in one
graceful move, dark brown eyes glittering fiercely.
"*You don't understand!*"

Two

A knock on the door saved her from the need to respond.

"Gena." Bertrand's rolling, English-accented voice called her through the door. "Gena, my dear, are you at home?"

"Yes, Bertrand, just a moment."

Jarrod's brow lowered into a frown. "Who's that? One of your admirers?" Gena glanced into the mirror to make sure everything was in place, then threw Jarrod what she hoped was an enigmatic smile. "One of my favorite people." She went to open the door.

"Bertrand! How did your taping for the commercial go today?"

A tall, thin, aesthetic-looking man with a flowing mane of white hair and a beaked nose, Bertrand favored her with his most put-upon expression. Unaware of the room's third occupant, he swept into it and thundered dramatically, "I can't begin to express how demeaning it was! They actually wanted me to get into a conversation with a cat. A *cat*! I ask you. *Me*, who once *auditioned* for the Royal Shakespeare Company, emoting with a cat! Life does not lay an easy path for a retired Shakespearean actor, Gena."

Grateful that he had interrupted her tense confrontation with Jarrod, Gena laughed. "It couldn't have been that bad, Bertrand. After all, you actually got to appear in the commercial. It's better than the usual voice-overs. What did they want you to talk about?"

He waved his hand with a flurry. "How should I know? Some nonsense about cat food, or mix, or chow. Meow, meow, meow! Needless to say, I'm vastly fatigued."

"I'm sorry you've had such a bad day, Bertrand."

"And that's not all! I must return tomorrow. They expect me and that revolting cat to have a meeting of the minds, as it were."

"Perhaps you'd like to sit down and join us."

Gena's gaze flew to Jarrod. He had resumed his position on the bed, appearing comfortably at home.

"Uh, yes. Bertrand, let me introduce you to Jarrod. He's . . . the new owner of my father's company."

Bertrand's white eyebrows climbed comically high. It was obvious—to Gena, at least—that he wasn't used to seeing a man on her bed. "Oh, I say! I *am* sorry. Do forgive me. I really didn't see you there. Perhaps I should come back later."

"No!" Gena grabbed his arm and steered him toward the love seat. "Actually Jarrod was about to leave. He was just in the area and dropped in to say hello." She glared at the man in question, who looked as if he had no intention of vacating his position on the bed. "Isn't that right, Jarrod?"

Jarrod smiled—quite insincerely, Gena thought. "No."

She had no idea how to handle the situation. Luckily another knock on the door gave her a moment's reprieve. Once again Gena answered it, standing back as Rose glided in on a cloud of sultry perfume.

Like Gena, Rose wore jeans, but hers fit her ripely curved hips in a way that left little to the imagination. Her remarkable cleavage showed to its best advantage in a scoop-neck kelly-green T-shirt that advertised Clancey's in a way Gena could never hope to.

One seeking the perfect example of how not to be a lady would find it in Rose. Gena's mother would have been horrified by her, but Gena found Rose delightful.

"Hi, Gena. Are you as tired as I am? If the lunch crowd gets any bigger, I'm going to insist that Clancey put on another waitress. Hi, Bertrand. How was the cat?"

"The beast urinated on me," Bertrand remarked glumly.

"That's too bad." Out of the corner of her eye Rose caught a glimpse of the room's other occupant, and her shoulder-length blond hair, bleached to platinum, whipped around. At the sight of Jarrod, her black eyes took on new life.

"Well, hel-*looo*, handsome! It's a little early for Christmas, but who's to argue with Santa Claus? Gena, introduce us."

Because the last thing Gena wanted was for Jarrod to get to know the people who had come to mean so much to her in her new life, she introduced the two with great reluctance. "Rose, this is Jarrod Saxon . . . one of my father's favorite people." She was running out of ways to introduce the man, she thought, her innate sense of humor temporarily getting the better of her. "Jarrod, Rose. Rose lives across the hall, and we work together at Clancey's."

Jarrod got up from the bed with a polished gallantry that left Gena gritting her teeth and had Rose throwing into gear her repertoire of feminine wiles.

He took her hand. "Rose, I'm so glad to meet you. Any friend of Gena's is a friend of mine."

"Oooooh! How nice for me. That will save a lot of time on boring preliminaries. We can get right to the good stuff. For instance"—her black eyes snapped flirtatiously, and both of her cheeks dimpled bewitchingly—"are you available?"

This time his smile was sincere, much to Gena's vexation. "That depends on what you'd like me to be available for."

"Oh, honey, are you ever somethin'!"

Gena had had enough. "Rose, was there something you wanted?"

"What? Oh . . . yes. I wanted to tell you that Clancey's been talking about putting in a salad bar. Can you imagine? A *salad bar*!"

"I can see it now. He'll probably want us to say to each customer, 'May I acquaint you with the salad bar?' Now I ask you, how does one perform an introduction between a human being and a piece of lettuce?"

"Look, Rose. I may not have worked at Clancey's as long as you have, but I hate these changes, too. Still, remember that for years Clancey's barely made ends meet. Now suddenly his bar is in fashion, and he sees a chance to make some money. We can't really object."

"Maybe you can't," Rose drawled, "but I sure can."

"I agree with Rose," Bertrand said. "Clancey's establishment should retain its integrity."

"Integrity doesn't pay the bills," Gena pointed out. Living on a waitress's salary had taught her much about the problem of making ends meet.

"Listen, don't let that little twerp fool you," Rose said, taking the opportunity to bat her false eyelashes at Jarrod. "That bar has provided Clancey with a steady income for years, and he's socked away plenty."

Jarrod couldn't restrain his curiosity. "Little twerp?"

"Clancey is only half-Irish, despite his name," Rose explained. "The other half is Chinese. Clancey looks Chinese. On the other hand, our big, red-headed bartender, Josh, is Polish, but looks like an Irishman. It makes Clancey's day when our new customers mistake Josh for him."

Jarrod's interest in her friends and her job made Gena distinctly uneasy. It was time for him to leave, she decided. She grabbed his jacket and shoved it into his hands. "Jarrod, it's been so nice seeing you again, but I know you have a plane to catch, so don't let us keep you." She opened the door and took his arm. "Give my regards to everyone back at Alexander's." Poised to push him out the door, she paused. "Or have you changed the name to Saxon's by now? Well, I suppose it doesn't really matter. Good-bye."

She succeeded in getting him into the hall only because he let her. But right before she shut the door, he turned and pinned her with his intense brown eyes.

"We're not through, Gena. I know where you are now, and I won't lose you again."

She slammed the door and leaned against it as if he were attempting to break it down.

Rose looked at her curiously. "Honey, you're as white as a little ol' ghost."

"Perhaps you should sit down," Bertrand suggested, alarmed.

She shook her head. "No, I'm fine. Really. It's just that seeing Jarrod again has brought back things that I thought I'd left behind."

Rose's black eyes took on a thoughtful expression.

"Have you known that chap long?" Bertrand asked.

"The problem is, I never really knew him at all." She pulled away from the door and walked to the love seat.

Rose threw Gena a sassy smile. "Hell's bells! I don't have to know him well. Five minutes with him is enough to convince me that I'd like to know him . . . better."

Bertrand smiled affectionately. "Really, Rose, you're such a wanton. Were I but twenty again, I would indeed make the effort to woo and win you."

"Aw, you know that no matter what age, you're still my favorite beau." Rose accepted his compliment with a toss of her platinum-blond head. "But let's be honest. I don't see how any red-blooded woman can look at that man without having obscene thoughts about his inseam!"

Gena groaned. "Listen, you two. I'm tired, and I'd really like to catch a nap before I have to go back to work. Do you mind?"

"Not at all, my dear. I, too, must recover from the tribulations of my day. Perhaps I'll see you later tonight. I may wander down to Clancey's for a pint of ale or two."

Rose grinned. "You mean a long-neck, don't you? That's all Clancey serves, for now, at any rate. Next week it'll be wine spritzers, sure as shootin'." As she walked out the door, she threw a last concerned glance over her shoulder at Gena. "You are looking a little pale. Get some rest, and call me if you need something."

"I will. Thank you, Rose. I'll see you later, Bertrand."

It took Gena less than a minute to strip off her clothes and climb into bed. Burrowing down under the covers, she closed her eyes, attempting to block the last hour from her mind.

It was no use. Jarrod had found her. Her eyes opened, and she stared up at the ceiling.

For autumn, the weather was extremely mild. Gena, however, felt cold. It was the same, terrifying chill that had gripped her body ten months ago as she had sat in the office of her family's lawyer and listened to him read her father's will.

Her father's death had been a shock. Gena hadn't even known he was sick until the last week of his life. He had kept the gravity of his condition from her, going about making plans for his daughter after his death just as he had done all her life. Gena couldn't help resenting it. If only she had known he was seriously ill! There was so much she would have liked to say to him. There was so much she would have wanted to do for him. But he hadn't given her that chance.

George Alexander had been a kind, eccentric man, who had single-handedly built a multimillion-dollar business. He was a man with "tunnel brilliance"; that is, his interest and capabilities were focused entirely on one narrow field: machine parts. That was what his company manufactured.

When it came to the everyday normal complexities of human relationships and living, though, Gena's father was lost.

Gena had had a privileged upbringing. She was the adored daughter, petted and protected. Unhappily, her mother, Nora, died while Gena was in college. Gena went on to graduate with a degree in business, and after a grand tour of Europe to satisfy her father, she settled down to work in the computer section of Alexander Manufacturing.

Jarrod Saxon was a business associate of her father's. As president of a small but steadily growing and prestigious design firm, he had won innumerable awards and much recognition for his innovative work. He collaborated closely with her father: Jarrod would design a product for a customer, either a machine part or an entire machine, and Alexander Manufacturing would then produce it.

Gena heard about Jarrod long before she met him. From her father she heard about this stellar young man, who was bright and ambitious and would go far in the business world. And from her father's secretary she heard rave descriptions that featured frequent references to the word *hunk*.

However, it wasn't until she met him at the annual Alexander's Christmas party that Gena became a believer. He was standing by the fireplace, and even through the crowd she could see how attractive he was. Then he turned and saw her. Without a word to the man he'd been talking to, he set his drink on the mantel and made his way through the crowd to her. Taking her hand in his, he led her into the adjoining room, which had been cleared for dancing. They danced three complete numbers before he asked her name.

From then on, things happened fast. By the end of the night Gena knew she was in love. Within a week she and Jarrod were lovers. Every spare moment they could manage was spent at Jarrod's apartment in each other's arms. There the world and its realities seemed far away. . . .

What a fool she had been! Gena rolled over and buried her face in the pillow. She had been young and in love, and she had believed that Jarrod loved her in return. After all, he had told her so often enough—during the long hours of their lovemaking.

It was their lovemaking that had at first blinded her, she decided. She had been swept away by their passion, by the intensity of their affair. But after a while she came to need more. They were lovers, but they weren't friends.

She had never considered herself insecure, but now she felt uncertain and vulnerable as she came to question whether there was substance beneath the passion. . . .

As carefully as she could, she began to question Jarrod, attempting to find out what went on inside him, what drove him. She got nowhere. He was such an intense man—and yet so closed. Her questions seemed only to make him uncomfortable, and as a result her insecurities grew.

Looking back on their weeks together she realized that the most personal thing Jarrod ever told her about himself was that he loved cookies-and-cream ice cream. Once, after they made love, he brought a half a gallon of the stuff to bed, and together they ate it. Later this became a routine—a little ritual they shared. One Gena had treasured.

But she now knew that she had been living in a fantasy world, where perhaps the only reality was their passion. And upon her father's death, that fantasy world came crashing down on her head. Not only did she have to deal with the loss of her father, but she had to deal with Jarrod's betrayal as well.

She learned of it at the reading of the will. As the lawyer's voice droned on, Gena sat beside Jarrod, stunned, as she found out that her father had left his company and most of his fortune to Jarrod Saxon. Up until that point she had assumed Jarrod's presence was only to offer her his support. She could still remember how tense he had been, and how all she could think of was that he had known all along! He must have.

That was when everything became clear to her. He had planned it all along. With the merging of the two companies, he would have more power than most men could even dream of. He had used her to get to her father.

The will was in her father's own words, and he said that Jarrod had assured him that he would take care of her for the rest of her life. He would die happy, George said, and join his dear Nora with the knowledge that Gena's future was secure.

As she sat in her chair in the lawyer's office, anger had quickly replaced Gena's bewilderment. A small portion of that anger had been directed toward her father. She had loved him, but it hurt her that he, however well-meaning his intentions, had put her in this position.

Most of her anger, though, was reserved for Jarrod. He had obviously been willing to promise her father the moon in order to get the company, and it had worked.

The lawyer finished the reading and discreetly left the room. Jarrod turned to her. "I'm sorry," he said. "I don't know what to say. We can work it out." She heard his words only from a distance.

Suffering from too much shock, too much pain, in such a short period of time, a terrible fury began building inside her. Still Gena forced herself to act calmly. She told Jarrod that she needed time alone, and he didn't argue. She drove home and packed a couple of bags. What money she could lay her hands on she stuffed into a purse. Then, without so much as a backward glance, she got into her car and drove away.

A day later she found herself in a small town in New England. There she sold her car, and caught the first bus south. For two days she rode the bus. Her mind was wonderfully numb. The passing scenery was a blur. But on the morning of the third day she awoke to find herself in a bus terminal in Dallas, Texas. She decided that she had run long enough.

Her first act was to rent a hotel room and read

the classified ads. She wanted something far removed from the job she had held in the computer section at Alexander's. Finally she found what she had in mind. A small bar in a rundown neighborhood needed a waitress. She took the job.

On her first night she met Rose, who mentioned that there was a room vacant in the house where she lived. The very next day Gena moved in.

The succeeding months hadn't been easy. There were times when she had thought she would go crazy, wanting and missing Jarrod. Those were her weak moments.

During her strong moments she had filled her life with her work and the people of the house and the neighborhood. And now she had a new life, one that she refused to let Jarrod Saxon destroy.

Gena awakened to loud noise. She lay still a minute, listening, but couldn't decide what could be causing the commotion on the stairs.

After a moment, curiosity got the better of her. She threw back the covers and reached for her thigh-length kimono. By the time she opened her door, the source of the noise had reached the landing.

"Jarrod!"

He had an overnight bag in one hand, and in the other he held several boxes. Behind him Sugar was dragging four shopping bags up the stairs.

"Oh, hi," Sugar called out gaily. "I'm sorry we

woke you up, but I've got great news. Your friend will be moving into our vacant room."

"My friend?" Her gaze switched to Jarrod in disbelief.

Jarrod remained silent.

Blithely unaware of any tension in the air, Sugar shook her head. "He didn't have much furniture, so we've been out shopping. I can't tell you what a good time we've had! Why, Jarrod insisted on only the best."

"I just bet he did."

Sugar beamed. "My Tex would have sure 'nuf approved. He believed in only the best too." She set down the bags she was carrying, fished for the key to the vacant room, and let out a happy laugh. "I've always wondered why Tex married me, although I *was* quite a looker when I was a young girl."

Jarrod supplied the expected response. "You're beautiful now, Sugar."

"Oh, I declare, aren't you the sweetest thing, though? Isn't he sweet, Gena?"

"I never thought of it that way. Sweet things make me sick."

"Really? That's too bad." Sugar's glance went from one to the other, finally settling on Jarrod. "I bet you're a romantic man, too."

"Why, yes, I am."

"No, he's not."

Sugar's eyes sparkled vivaciously; clearly she was enjoying this interplay her comments provoked. If there was one thing Sugar loved, it was romance. "But he must be, Gena. He told me himself he came all the way from Philadelphia just to be with you."

"Believe me, his reasons for coming here are anything but romantic."

Jarrod winked at Sugar.

"Oh, I just adore a good love story!" Sugar opened the door of the apartment that was next to Gena's and pushed the bags across the threshold. Instead of entering, however, she turned back to her new audience of one. "Tex and I shared a love that was something special, Jarrod, and I must tell you how we met. Years ago, as a young country girl, fresh from the South, I had a job as assistant to the wardrobe mistress for a Broadway show. Well, the leading lady had quite simply the *most* alarming bo-*zooms* I've ever seen." Sugar paused to hold her hands out in front of her chest by way of illustration. "One evening shortly after the show had opened, she literally split her seams and was left standing on stage in her knickers. Well, I tell you, Jarrod, you've never seen a woman throw such a fit. She tromped off that stage mad as a wet hen and came straight to me, blaming me for everything."

Sugar snorted. "As if I could have done anything to prevent it!" she went on. "That lady had been eating her way out of costumes throughout the rehearsals. Besides which, I don't know why she was so upset. Her striptease, such as it was, got the biggest round of applause in the whole play. At any rate, she was just about to give my

ears a good boxin' when a handsome man stepped
in out of nowhere and saved me! Tex. That man"
—Sugar sighed—"was a *real* man, if you know
what I mean. A *romantic* man."

Jarrod nodded his head sagely. Gena had heard
the story many times, and always paid attention
to each telling as though it were the first. But the
very elegant, hard-driving Jarrod had never struck
her as the sort to listen willingly, even patiently,
to the reminiscences of a woman with cotton-
candy hair wearing pink satin toreador pants.
Gena fully expected Jarrod to display the impatience she remembered so well—not the interest
he was now exhibiting. It had to be an act.

Sugar laughed. "Well, I had never seen Tex before, but it turned out he was one of the show's
'angels.' You know, one of the investors? Not only
did he protect me from the wrath of that terrible
woman, he married me, and brought me home to
Texas. We had a wonderful life, Jarrod, right up
to the time he passed on. That was about ten
years ago now."

"These years must have been lonely for you,"
Jarrod said.

Gena shook her head. His sympathy sounded
completely sincere. It irked her. What was he up
to?

"I *was* lonely, and I was also running out of
money. I was, that is, until I got the idea of turning our home into sort of a boarding house. Rose
came to live with me. Then Bertrand, and there
were others who didn't stay as long." She smiled

fondly. "Gena, of course, is my most recent ten-
ant. The girl has been a blessing to us all, Jarrod."

"Hadn't you and Jarrod better put away those
packages, Sugar?"

"Landsakes, yes! Imagine me out here on the
landing prattling away when there's work to be
done. Well, it just goes to show you, I guess. A
handsome face can still work wonders, even on an
old woman like me."

"I refuse to consider you an old woman, Sugar,"
Jarrod said gallantly. "You're *much* too attractive."

Sugar blushed all the way up to her spun-sugar
hairline. "Aren't you just the nicest man?" she
said in a crooning voice. "Don't worry about a
thing. Gena will come around. Now let's get you
settled."

"Jarrod, may I have a word with you?"

He acknowledged the coolness in her tone with
an arch of his eyebrow, but nevertheless his voice
was pleasant—teeth-gratingly so.

"Why, certainly, Gena. Sugar, I'll only be a minute. If you'd like, you can start putting things in
place. I know that you have impeccable taste. I
trust your judgment implicitly."

"Oh, *my*!"

"Give me a break," Gena muttered under her
breath.

Sugar was apparently so taken with Jarrod that
she floated euphorically into the vacant apartment.
Without a word, Jarrod followed Gena into hers.
The moment the door had closed, she wheeled on
him.

"What do you think you're doing?"

"I thought it would be obvious."

"It looks as if you're planning to move in. But that can't be! You're smarter than that."

He shrugged and crossed his arms over his chest. "I guess I'm not."

Gena let out a long breath. "Okay, Jarrod. I'm not up to playing games with you, so just tell me, what do you hope to gain by all this?"

"You." The one word, so simply spoken, carried an unexpected power.

"Not a chance!"

He reached out to touch a strand of her tousled hair. "Have I ever told you how beautiful you are when you've just gotten out of bed?"

He had. Many times. She jerked her head away and stepped out of his reach. "Stop it!"

It seemed to her that, just for a moment, his shoulders drooped. "All right," he said at last. "I'll tell you why I decided to stay. It was something you said, Gena. You said you didn't know me. I've decided to change that."

"*You've* decided."

"That's right."

She shook her head. "Whatever you're planning, it's much too late, Jarrod."

"I disagree."

Her mind raced. She was beginning to think that he really didn't know what she had been up to these past months. And if that were the case, maybe he wouldn't have to find out. If he went back home . . . if she stopped her activities right now . . .

"Jarrod, you own two corporations that together yield millions of dollars a year. Corporations of that size don't run themselves."

"I guess that's my worry," he said quietly. "Obviously I haven't stopped to figure out all the details yet. I'll meet each problem as it arises. But to tell you the truth, I'm hoping it won't be that long before you and I can resolve our problems and go home."

She didn't believe him, not for a minute. "What do you want?" she asked, her voice rising on a note of panic.

"I told you."

"No, no." She shook her head, dismissing the idea that he could want only her. She had believed that once. Never again. "There's got to be something else. Were there conditions that my father set up in his will, conditions that the lawyer didn't tell me about? Do you need to marry me to gain full control of the company?"

"There were no conditions. George took our marriage as a given."

She gave a bitter laugh. "Poor Dad. He was naive in so many ways. And so trusting."

"Maybe, but he knew me. Something I guess I didn't give you a chance to get to do. I rushed you into an affair, and it was so wonderful, there didn't seem any need for anything else." His voice softened. "Do you remember, Gena? Do you remember how sometimes we couldn't wait till we got to my apartment? How sometimes we had to stop along the road? And then when we'd finally get to my place, how we'd make love for hours and hours?"

"I remember everything, Jarrod," she said dully. "Does that make you happy? Proud of yourself? Fine. So be it. Now please leave."

"I'm not leaving, Gena." He took a step forward, and he was close enough so that he only had to whisper for her to hear him. "Every time you turn around, I'm going to be there. With or without your cooperation, I'm going to become your shadow."

She felt as if a fist were closing tightly around her heart. "For how long?"

"For as long as it takes. You and I are going to become so close, we'll wonder how we managed to breathe without each other for ten whole months."

Gena began to tremble. "Get out, Jarrod. Now!"

"I'll leave. For now. But before I do . . ." He reached for her, and his lips came down on hers in a kiss that, when it was finished, left her with a desperate need for more. . . .

Three

Clancey's was basically one large, irregularly shaped room, with a bar against one wall and the kitchen located behind the wall. A short, dimly lit hallway offered access to the kitchen and rest rooms.

Tables and chairs were crowded onto the cracked linoleum floor. The horn from a longhorn steer hung proudly over the bar. Several deer heads vied for space on the walls, along with various neon signs proclaiming the benefits of different types of beer—even though Clancey served only one kind: Lone Star.

Historically his menu had been equally one-dimensional. Clancey had a deer-hunting license in central Texas, and as a result kept a freezer full of venison. Venison chili had been a great favorite with the old crowd, but it had been politely ignored by the new people. In hopes of inspiring the palates of his new customers, Clancey, ever the optimist, had tried venison-sausage quiche. Unfortunately it had not been the success he had hoped.

Recently Clancey had hit upon something new. This was a marinade of bourbon, brown sugar, and chili sauce in which tiny sausages swam. Each sausage was stuck with a toothpick bedecked with a miniature cellophane pompom. Heavy on the bourbon, this concoction had become a great hit.

With experience born of ten months of on-the-job training, Gena cast a harried eye around the bar. The night wasn't going to be an easy one. The dinner crowd didn't seem to be thinning out. And to top it off her two least favorite people in the world had just walked in, separately.

Jarrod came in first. In Gena's grudging opinion he easily stood apart in this crowd of young men and women on their way up in the world. His self-assured air and understated elegance proclaimed that he had nothing to prove. And although she hated to admit it, Gena had a feeling that his confidence was inherent and would exist even were he not the head of two major corporations. She noted that there wasn't a person in the place who didn't heed his arrival, especially the women.

Like a heat-seeking missile, Rose zeroed in on him and seated him at an out-of-the-way table where he would have an excellent view of the whole room . . . and Gena.

The second man to enter the bar was Cole Garrett. His arrival always garnered a great deal of attention, and if it didn't, he would manage to do something to make sure heads did turn. He had a feature-perfect handsomeness and, in Gena's judgement, carried the successful look further in a wholly pretentious way. Outside in the parking lot, Gena knew his scrupulously clean and polished beige Mercedes 500 SEL waited for him, with its two-line, speaker car phone. She knew because he mentioned it to her every chance he got.

Since Rose was concentrating on Jarrod, it was left to Gena to seat Cole.

"How are you this evening, Gena?"

"Fine," she murmured, leading him to his favorite table, located in a prominent spot in the center of the room. "And you?" she asked politely, although she didn't really care. Cole was a real-estate developer who operated in the neighborhood, and there was something about him that had always made her uneasy.

"Never better." After taking the seat she pointed out, he carefully adjusted the cuffs of his monogrammed silk shirt so that no one would be able to miss the diamond-studded Rolex watch on his wrist.

Gena had seen him go through the same motions dozens of times. Dutifully she waited until he was finished before she handed him the most recent version of Clancey's much-revised menu.

Cole took it, looking around the room. "Clancey's

business is getting better and better. I'm very pleased. It's good for the area." He paused, switching his attention to her. "When are you going to break down and accept one of my dinner invitations, Gena?"

Since he issued one every time he saw her, Gena had been expecting this. It was one more thing the man had to get out of the way before he would give her his order. As nicely as she could, she smiled. "I'm not interested in going out, Cole. I've told you before. It would be better if you just stopped asking."

"I didn't get where I am today by accepting no for an answer, Gena. You'll change your mind."

Cole Garrett was much too smooth for her liking. "What can I get you tonight?"

His cold gray eyes flickered with annoyance, but he nodded his temporary acceptance of her change of subject, and settled down to study the menu.

From across the room Jarrod watched grimly as Gena spoke with the good-looking, well-dressed man. Surely she was spending more time with him than was strictly necessary. They seemed to know each other well, he noted. Too well. Jealousy gnawed at his insides, and he didn't even try to fight it.

Since they had been apart, he had been tormented by images of Gina with other men. Now he was seeing it right before his eyes. While he watched, she smiled at the man, and he had to force himself to remain in his chair. Jealousy was a primitive emotion, and it aroused a primitive and violent anger in him. He felt like tearing the man limb from well-dressed limb, but somehow he knew that if he did, Gena would never understand or forgive. And as it was, she had a lot to understand and forgive him for.

Still, he didn't stop watching the two until he saw Gena walk briskly past the bar and into the kitchen to hand in the order.

Settling more comfortably into his chair, he waited for Rose to return with his dinner and thought about his decision to stay in Dallas. True, it had been made on the spur of the moment, but once he'd realized Gena wouldn't return home with him, there had been little else he could do. Now that he had found her, there was no way he could leave her here. She was perfectly capable of picking up and moving on, and if she did that, he might not be able to find her again.

Jarrod saw Gena return from the kitchen and pause by the bar, flipping through her order pad. His gaze sharpened as he watched the busboy, a gangly youth who looked to be about nineteen years of age, sidle over and whisper something in Gena's ear. The look she gave the boy was filled with such tenderness that Jarrod had to fight back a fresh surge of jealousy. He was in a bad way, he thought with disgust, when he became jealous of a boy.

"How's it going, Peter?" Gena asked. She knew his family was in financial trouble. Peter's father had left when the boy was only twelve years old.

Since that time, Peter had been forced to hold down various jobs; in fact, he was the prime wage earner in his family. His younger sister was only nine, and his mother was handicapped. She had always had trouble finding work.

Peter grinned self-consciously. Gena was the nicest lady he had ever met, and the most beautiful. He still had a hard time believing she was really interested in him. But she was, and she was the only person he was comfortable enough with to talk to about his problems. "Mom's got a job interview tomorrow."

"That's great, Peter. I know how badly she's wanted to work."

Peter's grin faded. "It's important to her to contribute. She hates taking welfare. The bad news is, the company is located off the bus lines. A neighbor promised to take Mom to the interview tomorrow, but it's only a one-time thing. Mom needs a car that's specially equipped so that she can drive herself to work, and that's gonna cost money that we don't have."

"Perhaps the company will have some solution. Let's wait until we hear whether or not she gets the job before we start worrying." Gena smiled gently. "Your mother is a great lady, Peter, and I know you love her very much."

Peter blushed. "She deserves a lot better than she's gotten out of life, that's for sure."

"And so do you. If your mom gets a full-time job, then your salary will make it possible for you to go to college, at least part time, won't it?"

His young face twisted into an expression that held little hope. "If. That's a big word, Gena."

Gena patted his thin shoulder. "Don't worry, Peter. Something will turn up. You'll see."

"Hey, Gena. How about remembering your customers?" Clancey yelled.

On her way out of the kitchen with an order, Rose slinked over to Clancey's short, compact form, and in her sultriest voice she murmured, "We live to obey you, Clancey. You must know that."

Gena smiled as she saw Clancey gulp. No man was immune to Rose's charms, and she had long suspected that with the slightest of efforts, Rose could have Clancey wrapped around her little finger.

Later, as Gena emerged from the bathroom, she nearly bumped into Jarrod. "Excuse me." She tried to go around him, but he formed a solid obstacle. It seemed to her he practically filled the narrow hallway.

"I learned something tonight," he said.

"Education is a wonderful thing. Now, if you'll excuse me . . ." She tried to walk around him, but his arms came out to block her.

"I've learned that you are sexy as hell when you wear jeans and a T-shirt."

"I don't want to hear this, Jarrod."

He took a step forward, making her take a step backward, forcing her against the wall. "Every time you've bent over tonight, I've had to force myself to remain in my chair."

"I have work to do, Jarrod," she said, fighting

the weakness that was infusing her lower limbs. To get her mind off the insidious feelings, she looked over his shoulder and cursed Clancey for being so cheap that he refused to use a higher-wattage light bulb in the hall.

"I wasn't the only man looking, but I was the only man in the room who has the right to make love to you."

"That's not true—"

"All evening long I've had the greatest urge to step up behind you, pull down your jeans, and—"

"Jarrod!"

"Step between your legs . . ."

Lord, but the image his words invoked had kindled a fire that now spread rapidly in her stomach. What he was suggesting was outrageous and erotic, and she wanted it. "Jarrod . . ."

"Well, hi, sports fans!" Rose greeted them cheerfully. "Don't let Clancey catch you. He might want to charge admission."

"Rose, can you help me out here?" Gena asked, pushing against Jarrod's chest with a strength born out of embarrassment at her own weakness.

"Sure, honey." Rose reached out to lightly pinch one of Jarrod's buttocks. "I can tell you that this man has the cutest tush I've ever seen."

"Thanks, Rose," Gena muttered, glaring at Jarrod.

"Thanks, Rose," Jarrod said, grinning at Gena.

"No problem. Hey, can I recommend the bathroom? It's a lot more private than the hall. The fixtures provide some creative possibilities, although I must say the porcelain can be cold."

"No way." Gena put all her strength into one strong shove, and Jarrod released her.

"Ladies, ladies!" Clancey had appeared and was practically dancing with agitation. "There are hungry people out there, waiting to be served. What are you doing, standing here in the hall?

Rose slid over to Clancey, put her arm around his shoulder, and pulled him close to cushion his head against her full breasts. Then, in a voice guaranteed to make any man's blood pressure rise, she said, "We're discussing our favorite sexual positions. Tell me, Clancey, what position do *you* favor? I really would like to know . . ."

Clancey practically choked.

Later that night Gena climbed the stairs to her apartment. Outside she hesitated. A light showed beneath Jarrod's door. She gnawed on her bottom lip for a moment, then opened her own door and went in.

Once inside she carefully locked the door, crossed to the bed, and knelt down. Reaching beneath the hem of the bedspread, she closed her hand unerringly around the handle of what appeared to be an ordinary briefcase, and pulled it out. For a long time she stared at the case. Then slowly she pushed it back into its hiding place.

Being out in the fresh air, doing something

physical, felt good, Jarrod concluded. He had been working in an office seven days a week, eighteen hours a day, for so long, he had almost forgotten what fresh air smelled like.

His hands gripped the rake firmly as he swept the leaves into a neat pile. When he had volunteered to clear the yard of leaves for Sugar, it hadn't been an entirely selfless act. In truth, he hadn't been able to stand the thought of being cooped up in his room one minute longer. He still didn't know how he'd manage living in that small room for any length of time.

He had already made several calls back east this morning, arranging for things to run smoothly—he hoped—in his absence. Making arrangements for his second in command to take over the day-to-day running of the companies had been surprisingly easy, he recalled. Surprising because for as long as he could remember, Jarrod had had his head down, running for success. Succeeding had become a way of life to him.

But when the choice had become to try to get Gena back or continue with his high-powered, success-oriented life, it had been remarkably easy to make his decision.

Pausing, he wiped his hands down the legs of the new jeans he had bought this morning. He couldn't remember the last time he had worn jeans. To his way of thinking, jeans were for leisure, for knocking about. He hadn't had time for either for as long as he could remember. His dark brows drew together as he reflected that he would now have the time, and he wasn't quite sure how he felt about this prolonged inactivity.

Suddenly he got the feeling that he was being watched. He glanced around. A small boy, perhaps five years old, was leaning against a nearby tree, studying him.

Glad for the diversion, Jarrod stopped raking. "Hi, there. What's your name?"

"Bobby."

"It's nice to meet you, Bobby. I'm Jarrod. Do you live around here?"

"I live in that house over there." The boy jerked a thumb over his shoulder, indicating a house two doors away.

"Well, I guess that makes us neighbors. I just moved in here."

The child's eyes took on new light. "You moved in with Sugar?"

"That's right."

"She's neat. She bakes great cookies." The little boy studied him for a minute, then said, "Do you want to see my scar?"

Jarrod eyed him curiously. "Scar? Did you have an accident?"

"No, I had an operation." Bobby proudly lifted his T-shirt to show a red scar that arced from his breastbone to the side of his ribs. "It's all better. It doesn't even itch anymore."

Jarrod felt an immediate surge of sympathy. Bobby was an awfully little boy to have had to

undergo what had obviously been major surgery
It must have been a terrible trauma for the child
But then, Jarrod reflected ruefully, he knew bet
ter than anyone that kids had no control over
what happened to them. He had lost his father
when he was fourteen years old, and he was still
suffering the scars.

He knelt down beside Bobby. "That's a great
scar, all right. What happened?"

"There was something wrong with my heart for
a long time, and it kept getting worse. I couldn't
play or anything. Mommy used to cry a lot, be
cause she and Daddy didn't have the money to
pay the doctor to fix me. But one day we got a
check in the mail for just the amount the doctor
needed. Mommy said it was a miracle"—Bobby
shrugged—"but it looked just like a piece of paper
to me."

"Really?" Jarrod's brows lifted. "That was sure
lucky for you. Miracles don't happen every day.
You must be a very special little boy."

"That's what Gena says."

Jarrod lifted an eyebrow in surprise. "Do you
know Gena?"

"Sure. Everyone knows Gena."

"Is that right? Well, at any rate, I'm glad it's all
over for you."

"Me too! Now I can run and play just like the
other kids. Only they don't think . . ." His voice
trailed off, and his face clouded.

"They don't think what?" Jarrod prompted.

"They don't think I can play ball very well. But Gena says all I need is practice. Can you play ball? Gena can play real good." As he glanced over Jarrod's shoulder, his face lit up. "Hi, Gena!"

"Bobby, hi!" Gena was strolling up the walk, on her way home from picking up a few things at the grocery store. She nodded coolly in Jarrod's direction, but it was to Bobby she spoke. "What are you up to on a beautiful day like today?"

"Showing Jarrod my scar. He said it was a great scar."

"Well, it is."

"Yeah, and I told him all about the miracle."

Gena hoped her voice remained steady as she said, "That's terrific, Bobby. I've got to go in now, but I'll see you later."

"Gena." Jarrod called her name quietly. It stopped her in her tracks. "I need to talk to you."

She wanted to run. Instead, mindful of Bobby's watchful eyes, she turned back toward Jarrod. "Maybe later. I have some things to do." It was a lie, but she told it well, she thought. She hurried into the house.

Jarrod followed, and caught up with her in the entryway. "You can't run forever. Sooner or later you're going to have to listen to me."

Gena didn't like it when he got so close. It brought back too many memories, too many longings, and as a result it required a great deal of bravado on her part to say, "That was my problem, Jarrod. I listened to you and believed every word you said."

Tenderly he touched her face. "We will work this out, babe. Believe me." She shook her head, although she was uncertain why. "You look tired," he said. "You work too hard."

"I enjoy it."

"Maybe, but you still look tired. Aren't you getting enough sleep?"

Not since you came to town, she said silently. Aloud she said, "Of course."

Sugar stuck her cotton-candied head out the door of her apartment. "Oh, good. I see you two are getting along much better."

"Sugar—"

"Jarrod, I wanted to make sure that you knew about our Thanksgiving dinner, although you don't need an invitation. You're one of us now. But you will need to bring a dish of some sort."

"Sugar, I don't think Jarrod will be here—"

"Thanksgiving, did you say? Thank you, Sugar. I'll look forward to it."

The next two days were difficult. It seemed every time Gena turned around, Jarrod was there, keeping an eye on her. She became preoccupied with trying to guess what he was up to. Logic told her that sooner or later he would get tired of hanging around watching her, and go back to Philadelphia. But logic had little do to with the fact that her nerves were winding tighter and tighter with every passing day. . . .

Then, one evening after Jarrod had been in town about a week, something strange happened that had nothing to do with him at all.

Late for work, Gena was racing down the stairs, heading for the door, when a visitor emerged from Sugar's apartment. The visitor was Cole Garrett, and the sight of him brought her to an abrupt halt.

As smoothly as ever he murmured, "Gena, how nice to see you."

Confused, Gena regarded him. "Did you come to see me?" she asked. "I'm sorry, but I'm on my way to work."

"That's okay. Actually I was here to see your landlady."

"Oh?" Gena looked from Cole to Sugar, who stood in her opened doorway. "I didn't realize you knew each other."

Although her face was pale, Sugar's painted-pink lips twisted into an imitation of a bright smile. "We were just discussing a little business, dear. Nothing important."

"Business? What sort of business?"

Cole took Gena's arm. "My car's just out front. Why don't you let me take you to work."

She shook out of his grip. "I'd prefer to walk."

The smile on Cole's lips stiffened into a hard, cold line, making Gena want to shudder. "One of these days, and very soon, I think you'll change your attitude toward me."

"Really, and why would you think that?"

"Gena," Sugar piped up, a nervous tremor in her voice, "shouldn't you be getting to work?"

Unfortunately Gena did have to leave. But since she had never known Sugar to be this nervous, or upset, she hesitated. "Cole, if you're upsetting Sugar in any way, you're going to have to deal with me as well."

"I would love to *deal* with you, Gena. I think I've expressed that wish many times. As for Sugar, I've done nothing to upset her. I've only helped her out." He turned to the older woman. "Reassure Gena for me."

"Gena, honestly, there's nothing to worry about. You just go on, now."

Cole dusted a speck of lint off his immaculate jacket. "That's right. You see, Sugar and I have a few interests in common, that's all."

Gena left for work, but couldn't get the encounter out of her mind. Throughout her shift at Clancey's she thought about it. Cole visiting Sugar disturbed her, and she didn't know why. And of course Jarrod, glaring at her from what had become his usual table, didn't help matters.

Peter approached from behind. "Hey, Gena."

She jumped, clutching at her heart. "Don't *do* that, Peter!"

"Do what?" he asked, genuinely puzzled.

She shook her head, realizing that she was being ridiculous. Next she would be jumping at her own shadow. "Nothing. I'm sorry."

"Listen, I gotta ask you. Is that guy a friend of yours?"

She swiveled around to look, even though she knew exactly who Peter meant. "What guy?"

"That guy over there with Rose. He's been here every night this week."

Her gaze went unerringly to Jarrod, who was looking up at Rose, laughing at something the waitress had just said.

"He watches everything you do."

"Just ignore him," she advised.

"That's easier said than done. Those eyes of his practically bore into me every time I get near you."

She glanced back at Jarrod, and her eyes locked with his. The heat of his gaze from across the room threatened to undo the air of reserve she always assumed in his presence. Deliberately she turned her back on him. "Tell me how your mother's interview went."

"She got the job."

"That's wonderful, Peter! Why didn't you tell me?"

"Because . . . Well, it's not so simple. We're not sure she can take it. She still has that transportation problem."

"Did she check with the personnel department? Perhaps there's another employee who lives nearby, who could give her a ride."

"She did check, Gena. There's no one."

"Well, how about the company? Maybe they have special transportation available."

"She's checked that, too, and everything else she can think of. But she's the first handicapped person whom they've ever agreed to hire. It's evidently a test, of sorts. If Mom works out, then they'll hire more handicapped people. Also, Mom feels obligated to really pull her own weight with them so that they'll give other people like her a chance. The company gave her a week to decide, but so far she hasn't been able to work anything out."

The hopelessness in his voice wrenched Gena's heart. She raised a hand to his cheek. "Oh, Peter. Why didn't you say anything sooner?"

"What could you do, Gena? I mean—you could worry, too, along with Mom and me. But what's the sense in that?"

"Don't give up, Peter. Just don't give up, you hear?"

He gave her a shy smile. "Thanks, Gena. You know," he blurted out, "you're the only person I can talk to!"

"Peter!" Clancey yelled. "Tables five and eight need clearing, *if* you wouldn't mind!"

Rose glided by. "Oh, Clancey, you're *sooo* masterful!"

Clancey's blush extended up his neck, over his face, and past his receding hairline.

Giving Gena a last thankful smile, Peter hastened to his chores.

The next morning Gena pulled the briefcase from under her bed and opened it. Out popped the plasma screen; it was a component of the latest, most advanced, portable device for talking long distance to one's computer bank. Next she reached for the power strip she kept in the top of her closet and plugged it into the wall. Then she plugged the heavy power cable into the power strip and attached the lighter telephone line to the nearest phone jack.

As the terminal dialed the WATS-line number of the big mainframe at Alexander Manufacturing's computer center, Gena reflected that computers were wonderful things. And it was her knowledge of them and how Alexander's computer department ran that had given her the means to get back at Jarrod.

Once the idea had occurred to her, it had been incredibly easy to break into Alexander's computer system and gain access to their data files, more particularly the master file of charities to which Alexander Manufacturing regularly contributed.

From there it had been a simple matter of setting up a dummy charity, which, upon request, would funnel as much money as Gena deemed necessary into a bank account here in Dallas.

She keyed the date, time, and user identification, using Jarrod's personal number. Owing to her familiarity with the company's security structure, it had been ridiculously easy to reason out the codes that enabled her to sign on to the computer as Jarrod.

She paused, recalling the estimate that she had received from a local car dealership. She had explained to them the nature of Peter's mother's handicap, and they had in turn detailed the special equipment she would need and the price.

After the sign-on process was completed, Gena did not hesitate to key in the transaction for the relatively large amount of money required. Completing and verifying the transaction, she signed off and sat back with a sigh.

Within a day, two at most, the money would be wired into the Sherwood Preservation Society bank account. As soon as Gena received confirmation that the deposit was in the account, she would write a check to Peter's mother for the full amount for the car she so desperately needed, and put it in the mail. The check would be signed, "R. Hood."

Simple, Gena told herself, getting up to replace the innocuous-looking briefcase beneath her bed and the power strip on the highest shelf in her closet.

Sounds of Bobby's laughter drew her to the window. He and Jarrod were out on the front lawn, throwing a football back and forth. As she watched, Bobby heaved the ball with all his might, and Jarrod caught it easily.

Suddenly Gena became aware that her head was throbbing dully, and unfortunately the memory of how the Sherwood Preservation Society had begun didn't help the pain. A couple of months after she had begun living at Sugar's, she had met Bobby and his parents and learned of his illness. Her heart had gone out to Bobby, and she had cursed Jarrod that she didn't have the money to help the sick little boy.

That was when the idea had formed in her mind. The whole concept had immense appeal—robbing from the rich to give to the poor.

From there, things had gone fast and smooth. She had had just enough money left from the sale of her car to buy the little computer, and breaking into Alexander's computer system and setting up the bank account had taken only a short while.

She knew that at regular intervals independent auditors randomly selected files for review, and that if her charity were chosen, her theft would become apparent. Still, she felt that the odds were slim that her charity would be selected for such an audit. Regardless, she was willing to take the chance. What she wasn't willing to do was leave someone else open for blame in the event that the Sherwood Preservation Society *was* audited. So, just in case, she deliberately left an audit trail that would tell Jarrod plainly that she was responsible.

All in all, it had all been incredibly easy, and the new charity of the Sherwood Preservation Society had gone into operation.

She had helped quite a few people since. Every one of her "withdrawals" from Alexander's had been for someone exceptionally deserving.

She lay down on the bed and plumped a pillow behind her head. It was true that the idea had been conceived because of her anger at Jarrod, but it had continued because of her love of the people around her and the good that she was doing. During the past months, there had been times when the guilt over what she was doing had nearly gotten the better of her, and she had rationalized that the money she was taking should be hers anyway.

But deep in her heart she knew what she was doing was wrong. There was a word for her actions: Embezzlement.

Four

Gena tried to rest, but the shouts and laughter from outdoors, where Jarrod and Bobby played, soon had her on her feet again. Then, last night's encounter with Sugar and Cole Garrett was worrying her. Gena couldn't get it off her mind. The idea of Sugar and Cole talking about anything at all was just too weird. Granted, they had had a simple explanation, but it had been *too* simple. All her protective instincts had been aroused, and she found she couldn't leave the matter alone. If there was something going on between Sugar and Cole, she intended to find out what it was.

Gena wandered to the window to watch Jarrod and Bobby. Despite her determination to ignore Jarrod, she had to admit that she was fascinated by what she saw. Jarrod in jeans and a sweat shirt, playing football with a small boy, seemed totally out of character. But there he was, apparently enjoying himself as much as Bobby.

"Wait a minute, Bobby," Jarrod called. "I don't think you're holding that ball quite right."

Bobby ran to his side, and Jarrod knelt down so that the two were the same height. "See, your index finger, the one you point with, should be placed where the laces start, and your thumb goes underneath"—he positioned Bobby's hands on the Nerf football—"like this. Okay?"

"Okay!" Bobby answered happily. "That should help me throw better, huh?"

"It sure should." Jarrod happened to glance up, and saw Gena watching them. He grinned. "Look, there's Gena."

"Hey, Gena," Bobby called. "Why don't you come on down and play with us?"

"Yeah," Jarrod echoed. "Come on down and play with us."

Gena forced herself not to grind her teeth in frustration at Jarrod's ploy. He had *known* Bobby would want her to come down once he knew she was watching!

"Gena, please!" Bobby called. "You and I can play against Jarrod."

Casually Jarrod tossed the ball into the air and caught it, waiting, smiling. What could she do? Gena mused. Well, maybe the fresh air would clear up her headache, and even if it didn't, it would do her a world of good to tackle Jarrod and knock him on his provocative rear end.

"I'll be down in a little while," she promised. "I need to talk to Sugar first."

After casting one last look around the room to make sure she had removed all sign of her illegal activities, Gena made her way downstairs. She found Sugar in the parlor, brandishing a feather duster.

"Oh, good, Gena, there you are. I heard Jarrod and Bobby calling for you. I was hoping you'd go out and play with them."

"I'm going to in a minute, but first I want to talk to you."

With a lighthearted laugh Sugar waved the feather duster in Gena's face. "Don't tell me you need advice on how to handle that gorgeous man out there!"

"No, no. I wanted to ask you about last night."

"Last night?"

"Cole Garrett."

Sugar's smile vanished.

"Is he trying to buy this house from you?" Gena asked, knowing that there were times when being blunt was the only way to get anywhere with Sugar.

Dropping her gaze from Gena's, Sugar ran her fingers through the feather duster. "Why, no, that's not it at all. He just came by. . . ."

Gena took the feather duster away from Sugar, so that the older woman was forced to look at her. "You'd tell me, wouldn't you, if you were in trouble?"

"*Trouble*, why good gracious! Ole Mister Trouble has never bothered me one whit. My Tex always used to say, if things look black today, just wait until tomorrow, and they'll look much better."

"Tex and Scarlett O'Hara had a lot in common," Gena muttered.

"Is that so?" Sugar asked, obviously glad to change the topic. "Now, isn't that interesting? And I don't believe he even knew her!"

"Sugar, listen to me. Cole Garrett is a shark, and I don't trust him. Promise that you'll come to me if you need help."

"Help? Why, Gena—"

"Promise me, Sugar."

"All right, all right." Sugar snatched her feather duster back. "Now get on out of here and go play. I've got work to do."

Once she was outside, Gena's headache disappeared. She found the air invigorating and Bobby's excitement contagious. "Okay, buddy, what's the plan?" she asked, catching a toss from him.

"Let's try to tackle, Jarrod!" Bobby squealed with happiness, jumping up and down.

"Wait a minute," Jarrod protested. "That doesn't seem quite fair. It's two against one, you know."

"But you're big," Bobby pointed out. "Besides, Gena's just a girl."

"I beg your pardon?" she questioned archly.

Jarrod laughed. "I tell you what, Bobby. Why don't we practice the running patterns I've taught you? You take the toss from Gena and try to make it to Mrs. Johnson's tree over there before I catch you."

"Okay!"

For the next fifteen minutes, they did just that, until Gena became worried that Bobby was over-exerting himself. His little cheeks were flushed and his breathing was coming in ragged gasps.

"Come over here, Bobby," she called, trying to decide how to handle the situation without letting him know of her concern. She waited until he trotted over, then knelt down beside him. "You're getting too good for Jarrod. Let's try a different strategy. Why don't you throw the ball to me, and let me see if *I* can get it past him?"

Bobby grinned. "That's a great idea."

Gena signaled to Jarrod, who nodded, seeming to understand. Then, accepting Bobby's hand-off, she took off, her golden hair flying out behind her as she zigzagged across the lawn, around a bush, through the leaves, and straight into Jarrod, who took her down in one humiliatingly easy move.

Glaring at him, she got to her feet and brushed off her bruised bottom. "Okay, Bobby, we'll try something else."

And they did. Gena ran ten different routes, trying to get past Jarrod, but she succeeded in routing him only once. And then, she had a sneaking suspicion that Jarrod had allowed her to get by.

Gena knelt beside Bobby in their next huddle. "I'm bound to get him this time," she said.

"I don't know. He's awfully good. He's even better than Mike Devito."

"Who's Mike Devito?" Gena asked, deliberately

prolonging the conversation to give herself more time to catch her breath.

"He's the kid over on the next street who's captain of our neighborhood team."

"Oh. Well, don't worry. This next play will be Jarrod's defeat." She received Bobby's toss, put her head down, and began to run. She was determined not to be stopped. She was so determined, in fact, that she didn't even see Jarrod coming in on her blind side. The next thing she knew, she was flat on her back, staring up into his laughing brown eyes.

"Give up?" he asked.

"Not a chance."

He lowered his body until most of his weight was against her. The pressure was achingly familiar, and Gena couldn't stop the response that leaped within her.

"Get up, Jarrod."

"Come for a ride with me."

"No."

He shifted his weight so that she couldn't mistake the rigid masculine definition of his body. "We haven't been alone since the day I got here. We need to talk, Gena, and it's pretty hard to do it around here."

"We've got nothing to talk about."

"Yes, we do." He tangled his fingers in the tousled mass of her hair. "You're absolutely beautiful like this—with no makeup on, and leaves in your hair. . . ."

"Gena?" Bobby called.

"Give us a minute, Bobby." Jarrod said. He looked at Gena. "Well?"

"Are you going to get up?" she asked with not quite as much conviction as she had felt before.

"No."

"Gena, are you hurt?" Bobby asked, running up.

"I'm fine, honey. Jarrod's just playing another game." Her blue eyes clashed with Jarrod's stubborn brown eyes. "Oh, all right," she muttered. "But that's all we're going to do—talk!"

A small flotilla of sailboats skimmed the surface of White Rock Lake, and a lone paddle boat churned along at a respectable rate. The warm fall afternoon had brought out the joggers in full force, as well as the usual large crowd of observers.

Jarrod switched off the ignition of his car and swiveled on the seat to face her. He wasted no time in getting to what was on his mind.

"Gena, I never asked your father to change his will."

"You expect me to believe that?" Although his car was a large one, she felt confined; hemmed in.

"Yes, damn it, *yes*! Your father was a very sick man. We did talk, but I never guessed what he was planning to do."

"Don't tell me. You only discussed the weather."

"Okay, I admit that we did talk about the future of the company," he said with reluctance. "Our ideas had always seemed to mesh. You know that.

We got along well. Your father felt he could trust me where business was concerned."

"That much is obvious, Jarrod." It still hurt that her father hadn't trusted her.

"We also talked about you, but at the time I didn't see the significance of that conversation. I thought that as soon as he was feeling better, we could talk further and I could find out what was really on his mind. Then, of course, it was too late."

"Not for you. You were made an extraordinarily wealthy and powerful man."

"And you ran." His eyes flashed in a way that told her Jarrod felt she wasn't the only one with a grievance. "You tried and convicted me without benefit of a jury. That was very hard for me to take."

For some indefinable reason, Gena was beginning to feel uncomfortable with her anger. "I wasn't wrong," she insisted. "The very first time I ever heard your name, I heard the word *ambitious* linked with it."

"I've never denied that I'm ambitious."

"And impatient to achieve your goals."

"If impatience is a fault, then I'll claim it. But you've got to give me credit for having some feelings, Gena. Imagine how I felt when I discovered you had disappeared. My first thought was that something had happened to you. But when there were no signs of foul play, and a servant said he had seen you drive off with a suitcase, I realized that you hadn't trusted me enough to talk things over. It was left to me to tell your friends and coworkers that you had taken a long vacation."

"And of course no one thought to question Jarrod Saxon."

"Do you think you were the only one grieving, Gena? I had quite a lot to deal with, myself. The woman I loved had left me without a word."

Gena squirmed uncomfortably. "Do you blame me?"

"You better believe I do. I was as stunned over the contents of your father's will as you were. I didn't have any idea what to say to you. But it didn't once cross my mind that we couldn't talk things out. You knew your father. You knew what he was like."

Yes, she knew, she thought dully. In her less-angry moments, she had admitted to herself that leaving the company to Jarrod was a fairly typical move.

George had seen that she was in love with Jarrod and had learned that he was dying at about the same time. His leaving the company and the money to Jarrod was an old-fashioned gesture that was quite out of touch with reality—but then, that was her father. It was his way of insuring that Gena would be taken care of after he was gone.

He had never been able to accept that she was anything other than his adored little girl. In his view, her education and expertise in the field of computers were all very well, but nothing could replace a husband who would love and cherish her.

"You're right, I knew my father. But it doesn't alter your role in getting him to change his will." She dragged her fingers through her hair and found it loose. She wished it were neatly plaited. Somehow, having it unbound and free-flowing made her feel more vulnerable, maybe because she remembered the many times in the past Jarrod had run his fingers through it. "And why are we even discussing it? What my father did and why— and the part you played in his decision . . . it doesn't matter anymore. I don't want the company. I'm happy."

Her gaze left him and focused instead on the shimmering water before them. Looking at the lake was easier! It didn't look back at her as if it wanted something from her—or as if it were somehow disappointed in her. What an absurd thought. "And you should be happy too," she went on heatedly. "After all, you now have exactly what you wanted all along, and you no longer have to sleep with the boss's daughter to get it."

"What if I want to?" He jerked her to him. Their faces were very close; she could feel his breath against her lips. Then his mouth came down on hers in a kiss of fierce desire.

It was just so damned easy to open her mouth to his, to allow his tongue to dip and delve, to meet it with her own. Her fingers slipped up his neck and into his hair. Oh, it was all just so damned easy! But too much time had passed. Too many things had happened. She pulled away, and, much to her consternation, found her breath coming in hard gasps.

His gaze slid hungrily over her reddened lips, and the look in his eyes told her he hadn't gotten nearly as much as he wanted from her. The expression in his eyes shook her nearly as much as his kiss had.

"You know, Gena, I think you figured that we were so good in bed, it was all we had. And maybe you were right, I don't know. Lord knows, I've never been an expert at relationships. I've never had the time. But now I'm taking the time, and whether you want to or not, you and I are going to get back what we had."

Angrily she shook her head. She couldn't allow herself to believe him! Because if she did, she would have to let him back in her life. And that could lead to even more pain.

"What's the matter, Jarrod? Are people back home giving you a bad time? Are they asking awkward questions? 'Where is Gena? Isn't it strange that Jarrod inherited what should have been hers, and now she's nowhere to be found? Do you think he killed her?' "

His hand circled her throat, and she couldn't repress the thrill that shot through her at his touch on her skin. "There's a thought," he said softly. "When I saw you walking home from work that first day and I remembered the hell I'd been through these last ten months—wondering if you were alive or dead, wondering whether you were sick and needed me, wondering whether you had found someone else and no longer thought of me at all—violence was a very real possibility. I had devoted every ounce of energy and power I possessed to finding you, and when I finally did, I couldn't decide whether to kill you or to make love to you." He smiled, and the effect of the smile went straight through Gena, making her shiver. "Actually, the choice was very easy."

"Jarrod, I can't see what you hope to gain by all this."

His fingers stroked her throat. "I want you to admit that I didn't deliberately set out to steal your father's company."

Exhaling a long breath, she put her hand on his wrist and pulled it from her throat. "The result is the same, no matter how it came about. Isn't that right?"

"And I want you to tell me that you still love me."

"There was never any love between us. What I saw as love was only lust."

"And I want you to come back home with me."

"This is my home now."

"Where we'll be married."

That stopped her. Not the idea that he wanted her to marry him. She was sure their marriage would make his life a lot easier. But the very thought of being his wife made her heart beat faster. . . . Much to her discomfort, she had to admit that their lovemaking on the day of Jarrod's arrival had reawakened needs she had thought successfully buried. . . .

She had to remind herself that to desire him was very destructive. If she wasn't careful, a certain look, a particular touch, would be enough to make her want to forgive him everything. To go back with him, so that they could resume their lovemaking, every night, every morning, any time of the day or night . . .

Even now, with him so close, she felt herself grow short of air. She rolled down the window to allow the breeze to reach her, so that she could think more clearly.

She had been hurt; her love had been shaken. But the thing was, she knew her father, and she knew he was completely capable of doing things just the way Jarrod had described.

Even so, giving Jarrod a second chance was not so easy as it seemed. There were things that Jarrod didn't know. And right now she could think of no way to tell him.

She opened the car door and got out. She heard Jarrod's door open behind her.

Leaning against the hood of the car, she waited until he was beside her. "Is there something you haven't told me, Jarrod? Is there some other reason why you've come to get me?"

He looked at her strangely. "I've told you everything."

She kept her eyes focused on the distant bank while she wondered how life could get so screwed up.

"Gena, come back with me."

His voice betrayed his frustration. She remembered that his level of patience had always been low. "I can't. At least not now."

There followed a lengthy silence that threatened to unstring whatever composure she had managed to hold on to until now. Finally, with genuine curiosity, Jarrod turned to her. "What is it here that makes you so happy?"

"You wouldn't understand."

"Try me. Please."

Why not? she thought. Maybe if he understood, he would go back to Philadelphia and leave her alone. "Okay. I grew up under privileged circumstances. I had many advantages, but in the end it brought me heartbreak, because the two people I loved the most let me down. Here life is simple. The people are honest. They're not after anything I have, because I don't have anything. It's a wonderful feeling. They like me for who I am on the inside. I'm not ready to go back, Jarrod. I'm not sure I ever will be."

This time his silence lasted even longer. "Then I'm going to stay."

She tried to tamp down her alarm. "You'll never make it here, Jarrod. It's not the fast-paced, high-powered life you're used to."

"Maybe not. Still, if you'll give us a chance, I will make it."

"A chance? What do you mean?"

"I mean I want you to give us a chance to get to know each other. Agree that you won't run automatically in the opposite direction every time you see me. And I also mean that I want you to promise you won't run away again. That you'll stay here too."

"It won't work. Don't you see, I thought we did know each other!"

"Exactly! So did I. It doesn't lessen what we had, to admit that we may not have known each other as well as we thought. All relationships have to be worked at. You build on them, day by day, and that's what I want us to do."

His words were hitting nerve centers all over Gena's body, making her want to believe him. And that weakening in her attitude toward him scared her. . . . She struck back. "*You* want us to—"

"Stop it, Gena, please. Just relax a little of that defensiveness, and admit that what we had wasn't all bad. What we need to do now is build on what we had, to make it more substantial."

While Gena didn't underestimate her own intelligence, she had also been forced to admit to a highly impetuous nature. She had rushed into her affair with Jarrod, blinded by her desire for him. Reason had told her over and over again to take a giant step away from him, to slow their relationship down. To let it develop more gradually, so that their love might have a more solid footing.

But once she'd heard the will read, she'd known it was too late. All her deep-seated insecurities had rushed to the fore, and her impetuous nature had led her to run. Her pride had been given a severe blow, and she still had a lot of anger to deal with.

And she had an even bigger problem. That same impetuous nature had led her deep into the game of dishonesty and fraud.

Well, she was tired of acting first and reaping the consequences later! Whatever the outcome, she knew she could no longer run.

She let out a long breath. "I'll stay, Jarrod. Beyond that I can't promise anything."

He nodded. "I'll accept that . . . for now."

Despite the fact that she, Peter, Clancey, Jake and the bartender, had handled the late Friday crowd alone, it had been a good night at work, Gena decided as she climbed the steps to the house. Things had gone smoothly, even with Rose absent.

Rose had started to leave three hours early on Friday nights—so she could watch "Miami Vice." That Clancey let her, spoke volumes to Gena concerning how the man felt about Rose. Clancey wasn't alone, though. Most men lost their heads over the flashy platinum blond.

Gena smiled, letting herself in the front door, then remembered that Jarrod hadn't been there either. That was a bit strange, since, whenever she was on duty, he could be counted on to be at what everyone now considered "his table." She had gotten so used to his presence that his absence had thrown her off balance. Not, of course, that she cared whether he was there or not, she told herself.

Gena looked into the parlor, to see Rose, Sugar, and Bertrand gathered around the television, deeply engrossed in an old horror movie. Jarrod wasn't with them.

"Hi, guys, how's it going?"

All three television viewers jumped in their seats. "Landagoshen, Gena!" Sugar exclaimed. "Don't creep up on a person like that."

"I'm sorry. Is the movie that scary?"

"Inane would be the more appropriate word." Bertrand looked down his long nose at her. "Why everyone in these horror films persists in going down to the basement alone to investigate strange noises when they should be exiting the premises immediately is beyond me. Shakespeare never would have allowed one of his characters to act in such a foolhardy manner."

Rose grinned at him. "I'm with you, honey. The first time my tub of butter says, 'Parkay,' I'm out the door."

Gena leaned against the doorframe, wanting to ask where Jarrod was, but not sure how to work it casually into the conversation. "So how was 'Miami Vice' tonight?"

"Wonderful!" Sugar bounced up and down on her chair cushion in her enthusiasm. "Everything on that show is so *pretty*!"

Gena grinned. "I know. Even the dead bodies."

Sugar's giggle resembled that of a little girl. "I don't know how they do it. I honestly think that the producers must tint the ocean to match Don Johnson's T-shirts. Can't you see it? Right before they get ready to shoot a scene, these production people go out in boats with giant bottles of food coloring?"

Rose scooped up a handful of popcorn and stuffed it in her mouth. "Oh, who cares about the ocean! I didn't even know there *was* an ocean in the show until you mentioned it just now. I've never seen anything but Don Johnson."

Bertrand shook his white head. "Personally, I think all the dither over him is much ado about nothing. The young man is devoid of any fashion sense. He wears T-shirts with suits, and suits that aren't pressed properly, at that. *And*"—Bertrand paused dramatically, as his eyebrows rose—"he wears no hosiery whatsoever!"

Rose rolled her black eyes in ecstasy. "He's got the sexiest ankles, doesn't he?"

Gena had heard enough about Don Johnson. Unable to find a subtle way to introduce Jarrod into the conversation, she went for the direct approach. "I don't suppose anyone has seen Jarrod?"

"Isn't that interesting how her mind jumped right from Don Johnson's sexy ankles to Jarrod?" Rose asked. "Tell me, Gena, does Jarrod have sexy ankles too?

Gena didn't know how to answer that, since Jarrod's ankles were the one part of his anatomy that she had never gotten around to studying. Fortunately Bertrand saved her.

"My dear Rose, you would accomplish so much more if you thought a trifle less about sex."

"Well, at least I only *think* about it most of the time, more's the pity!"

"Poor Jarrod is upstairs working," Sugar said. "I don't think he even had dinner."

"Working? What kind of work?"

Bertrand's thick white eyebrows raised in surprise. "Why, my dear, didn't you know? He's been receiving packets of work expressed from Philadelphia. The chap works bloody hard."

"I didn't know." Gena frowned, then realized that three pairs of curious eyes were trained on her. "Well, I guess I'll go on up. I'll see you all later."

Five

Slowly Gena climbed the stairs. Since Jarrod had moved in, she hadn't given much thought to how he was managing his two corporations. He hadn't mentioned this either. Meanwhile she had taken his virtually constant presence at Clancey's as an irritant. But tonight, with his regular table empty, the evening had seemed somehow flat. . . . And she found this situation very annoying!

She told herself it was curiosity that was drawing her toward Jarrod's apartment. Nothing else. And maybe she wouldn't even try to see him tonight. Maybe she'd just go on to bed.

But once on the upstairs landing, she passed her door and went directly to his. She had to knock twice before he answered.

"Gena, how nice!" Although he didn't show it,

Jarrod must have been surprised to see her at his door. He had lived in the house for several weeks now, and she had never been in his room.

In fact, Gena shared his surprise. And now that she stood face to face with him, she wasn't sure why she had come. Fortunately his easy smile went a long way toward erasing the awkwardness she felt.

"Come on in. You look tired. Did you have a busy night?"

"No more than usual," she said, crossing the threshold and wondering why she was doing it. "Of course Rose wasn't there to keep Clancey in line, so there was a little more yelling than usual." She shut the door behind her and turned just in time to see Jarrod's face crease with disapproval.

"I've seen how hard he works you, and I don't understand why you put up with it."

She had to grin. "Clancey's not so bad; he's just excitable. His bark is far worse than his bite, believe me."

As she spoke, she glanced around his room and was barely able to hold back a gasp at what she saw. It was furnished with just the bare essentials—an unpainted iron bed, a chest of drawers badly in need of refinishing, one raggedly upholstered armchair and ottoman, and a desk, of sorts, that was constructed from two sawhorses and a door. A lamp with no shade sat on the desk. Its base was an aqua-colored ceramic, open-mouthed trout. Its bare bulb was the only light on in the room. Papers were strewn everywhere. Where were all the top-of-the-line items Sugar had proclaimed he'd bought. Well, the sheets did look nice. . . . Jarrod's purchases had apparently been implements and accessories that were stored away—not furnishings. Never in her wildest imagination would Gena have believed that Jarrod would live in a place like this!

"Uh . . . I'm sorry. I'm obviously interrupting something."

"Just paper work, and it's a welcome interruption, believe me. Let's see"—he cast a quizzical glance about the room—"let me find you a place to sit down. What about the chair? Despite its looks, it's very comfortable."

"I'm sure it is," she said, hoping to keep the doubt from her voice. He perched on the overturned crate that served as a desk chair, while she settled into the armchair, shifting until she found a position where she couldn't feel the sharp edges of one threatening spring. "Jarrod, Sugar said she didn't think you'd eaten dinner."

His mouth twisted into a grin. "She's right. This work has to go out first thing in the morning, so I stayed in tonight to get it done. Did you miss me?"

She decided that to answer him might put her on the defensive, so she ignored his remark. "You know, when you decided to stay, I assumed you had delegated your authority to someone else."

"Oh, I did. But there are certain things that still require my attention." His lighthearted voice reflected complete unconcern. "Don't worry about it. I'm managing."

How different he sounded from the man she remembered in Philadelphia! she reflected. This laid-back guy bore little resemblance to the career-oriented man she had known. She wondered if she could rely on this new man. She wondered if she wanted to.

The room was quiet. With only the one light on, the shabbily furnished room had taken on an intimate air. A breeze came in through an open window, and as if this were its sole occupation for the evening, it lazily caught up the lace curtain, so that it fluttered gently and steadily. She should go, Gena decided.

"What about you?"

She jumped. "What?"

"Have you had dinner?" Jarrod was smiling at her with such tenderness that she began to wring her hands nervously.

"Oh, sure. I usually grab a bite whenever I get a minute at Clancey's."

"I've watched you, Gena. You hardly ever get a minute. I've also noticed that you seem to have an aversion to venison."

Gena nodded and chuckled. "I can't help it. When I was a little girl, my favorite movie was *Bambi*."

Jarrod rose from the crate and came to sit on the ottoman by her feet. His voice was as soft as the breeze flowing through the window. "I wish

I'd known you when you were a little girl. What were you like then?"

She moved uncomfortably. How had they skipped from the subject of Jarrod's missing dinner to her childhood? she wondered. "You don't want to know—because you wouldn't believe it."

"Why do you think I wouldn't believe you?"

"Because you never dug far enough to discover that part of me. You never even tried."

"Have I been that insensitive?"

The pain she thought she heard in his voice forced her to be honest. "It was probably as much my fault as it was yours."

"I definitely want to know about you, Gena." His voice coaxed. "Tell me."

Gena rarely thought about the child she had once been. It was too painful! None of her dreams had come true, and she supposed that was what hurt most of all. . . .

"Please," he prompted.

"Well," she began slowly, "believe it or not, I was like most other little girls. I had a whole nursery full of baby dolls, and I lavished care and love on them, dreaming of the day when I would hold my own babies in my arms. When I was a teenager, I spent the usual number of hours giggling with my girlfriends, fantasizing about the boys we went to school with, wondering what it would be like to be married. I just knew that somewhere there was the perfect man waiting for me." She stared at him defiantly. "So you see, I'm just like every other girl turned into woman. I had dreams."

"*Had*."

"Had. Like building castles in the air, it's dangerous to put any faith in them."

He took her hands in his. "I'm sorry," he murmured.

Her blue eyes reflected her surprise. "For what?"

"I'm sorry I've hurt you so badly. As apparently I have. I want to make it up to you, if you'll let me."

She pulled her hands from his. "You can't change what's happened."

"No, nothing can change the chain of events that began in that lawyer's office, but I'm hoping we can go on from here, with a love that's deeper and stronger for what we've been through."

A love that was deep and strong, a love that she could depend on . . . Was that remotely possible? she wondered.

A loud banging on the door interrupted the silence that had begun to stretch between them.

"Jarrod, Jarrod!" Sugar called through the door.

With a lingering look at Gena, Jarrod went to the door and opened it.

Alarmingly, Sugar's face was the exact color of her hair. "Oh, Jarrod, come quick! There's an awful fight going on downstairs." She grabbed Jarrod's arm and pulled him out the door.

"Who in the world is fighting?" Gena asked, following them.

"Oh, it's that Donny Joe Stevens," Sugar explained as they all hurried down the stairs. "You know what a bully he is when he's been drinking.

Well, he's been drinking, and since Rose wasn't at work when he got there, he decided to come over here and badger her. Bertrand took offense at some of the things Donny Joe said, and challenged him to a duel."

"A duel!" Jarrod momentarily lost his balance, but he quickly recovered.

"What are they using as weapons?" Gena asked, not nearly as surprised as Jarrod. She knew Bertrand's outdated code of chivalry and sense of propriety. But then of course, everything about Bertrand was outdated.

"I'm afraid all Bertrand has is his walking stick. Donny Joe, of course, has those ham hocks he calls fists."

As soon as they reached the downstairs landing, they heard the commotion on the lawn. Once outside, Gena's worst fears were confirmed.

There was Bertrand, wielding his walking stick as if it were the sharpest of swords, quoting Shakespeare at the top of his lungs. " 'Away, you scullion! you rampallion! you fustilarian! I'll tickle your catastrophe.' "

"*Henry IV, Part 2*," Jarrod murmured. "Very nice, but I doubt if it's going to get the job done."

"Donny Joe, you big, obnoxious clod, leave him alone and get out of here!" Rose was clinging to Donny Joe's back, her legs wrapped around him, her fists flaying at him, trying to prevent him from hurting Bertrand.

"Aw, Rose"—he swatted at Bertrand's walking

stick as if it were a fly—"all I want to do is see your rose tattoo. I bet it's so pretty."

She hit him again. "*No one* sees my tattoo, you cretin, unless I want him to! Not even my mother!"

"You've got a mother!" The idea was obviously novel for Donny Joe. He stopped swatting at Bertrand and turned his head to look back at Rose, thus giving Bertrand the chance to execute a nice thrust at Donny Joe's beer belly.

The next sound that came out of Donny Joe's mouth seemed to Gena a cross between a bear's growl and a lion's roar. Preparing to make mincemeat out of Bertrand, Donny Joe shrugged Rose off his back and swung his fist.

Jarrod stepped in between the two men just in time to catch a powerful right hook to his jaw and a left to his stomach. Before Jarrod could come back at the man, Gena, Rose, Sugar, and Bertrand all jumped on the hapless Donny Joe, alternately hitting him and berating him.

Donny Joe, deciding discretion was the better part of valor, finally broke free and lumbered off at top speed toward his pickup truck.

Gena went to Jarrod immediately, and nearly fainted at the sight of blood streaming from his mouth. "Oh, dear Lord, look at the blood. Jarrod, Jarrod, speak to me! Are you all right?"

Jarrod's most significant injury was to his dignity, but he decided it wouldn't hurt at all to let Gena fuss over him, so he held his stomach and didn't say anything.

Rose obviously had seen more than her share of

fights. "He's going to have a beauty of a colored jaw in the morning, and his stomach won't feel too good for a while, but he'll recover," she said matter-of-factly. "Bring him into the parlor, and we'll slap some ice on that jaw."

"I think we should take him straight to the emergency room," Gena insisted, remembering the horror she had felt when Donny Joe's fist had connected with Jarrod's face.

"That's not necessary," Jarrod protested, "but a good, stiff drink might help."

"Jarrod," Sugar exclaimed, holding the front door open, "you're a hero! You did just what my Tex would have done."

"I hope Tex would have done it with a little more success," Jarrod mumbled as they helped him into the parlor.

"I still think you ought to let a doctor check you over," Gena said, helping Jarrod to the settee.

Bertrand sank into a nearby chair. "I say, Jarrod, that was quite decent of you to step in like you did, but really not at all necessary. I had the chap on the run, you know."

Now lying down, Jarrod was afraid to comment. His jaw had begun to throb, and he had discovered that Rose was right. His stomach felt as if a 747 jumbo jet had rammed into it. Until tonight his fighting experience had been limited to bloody battles with his board-of-directors. Texas was proving to be quite an experience, in more ways than one.

Sugar patted Bertrand's shoulder. "A girl couldn't have a better protector. You were wonderful!"

"Thank you, madam."

Gena knelt beside Jarrod and took his hand. "You were such a fool. What on earth were you thinking of? That man could have killed you."

Rose entered the room bearing a kitchen towel filled with ice cubes, and caught Gena's last remark. "So help me, if that big lug put a permanent scar on that handsome face of yours, Jarrod, *I'll* kill *him*."

Jarrod started to laugh, and instantly regretted it.

Taking the ice from Rose, Gena placed it gently against his bruised jaw. "I think I should stay with him tonight," she told the others.

Surprised, Jarrod opened one eye, but he was wise enough not to say anything.

Sugar beamed. "Well, of course."

Bertrand nodded. "A veritable Florence Nightingale, nursing the warrior after a battle."

Rose snorted. "Since when does a lady need an excuse to spend the night with a brown-eyed, handsome man?"

"Excuse?" Sugar asked, amazed. "You mean she hasn't . . . they haven't . . . ? Gee, I just thought, what with their apartments being so close and all . . ."

"Never mind," Gena said firmly.

Gena couldn't sleep. Not only did she fail to find

a position where the damned spring didn't poke her through the threadbare upholstery of the chair, but she found it intensely irritating that Jarrod seemed to be sleeping with no trouble at all. And he was the one who was supposed to be in pain.

Still she couldn't help but be worried about him. She had never seen one man hit another, and she had been extremely frightened. In retrospect, she recalled that Rose and Sugar hadn't seemed nearly as upset. Gena supposed that by comparison she had led a sheltered life. But if anything had happened to Jarrod, she couldn't have stood it!

She peered over at his still form. She had left the bathroom light on with the door cracked open slightly, so that a thin beam of light illuminated Jarrod. A sheet and a chenille bedspread covered him now, but she remembered that he had insisted on getting undressed before he got into bed, and that all he had on was a pair of briefs.

She squirmed, lifted her bottom, repositioned herself, and—"Ouch!"

"What's the matter?" Jarrod asked softly.

"The spring just got me," she said before she thought to wonder why he was awake.

"Come over here."

Instantly she was on her feet and by his side. "What's the matter? Does anything hurt?"

"No." He reached for her hand and tugged until she was sitting on the bed beside him. "But I can't sleep either."

"Why? Do you need something? Aspirin? A drink of water? More ice?"

"I can't sleep because I keep watching you."

"I was moving around too much, wasn't I? It's just that the chair is so uncomfortable I don't know how you stand it."

"Sleep with me."

In the semidarkness she could make out his features clearly, but she couldn't see the expression in his eyes. A stab of suspicion pierced her mind. "You know, I think you're just fine now and can probably do without me."

"Never."

"I'll be just one door down the hall."

"But what if I need something?"

"Knock on the wall."

"You're heartless."

"And you're a fake."

She stood up, and was halfway to the door when she heard him moan. "Jarrod, what's wrong?" She was beside him again, anxiously hovering. "Are you in pain?"

In answer, he loosed another agonized moan.

"Oh, Lord, Jarrod, what can I do?"

"My mother used to kiss me till I was better."

"What?"

"Kiss me better. You know. Like here, where it hurts so badly." He pointed to his jaw.

She sat back down beside him. "You're terrible."

"Just desperate. And I hurt. I see no harm in giving it a try."

Because she was so relieved that he wasn't so

badly hurt, and because she realized that she really liked sitting beside him in these hushed hours of the middle of the night, Gena decided to humor him.

"Oh, all right." She leaned over him and placed a gentle kiss on his bruised jaw. "How's that?" she asked, raising back up.

"Okay, I guess."

He sounded remarkably like a little boy, Gena thought, amused. But she had every reason to know he was a man, a masculine, virile one.

"But I hurt here too." He threw back the covers and pointed to his stomach. His *naked* stomach. His briefs rode low on his hipbones, so that in the dim light she could make out the dark hairs that grew across his abdomen, continued to his navel, and disappeared beneath the waistband of his briefs.

"Forget it, Jarrod."

"My mother also used to cuddle me whenever I got hurt."

"She never did that!"

"I'm sure I remember feeling much better when she'd let me climb in bed with her and cuddle."

"I see. And do you also happen to remember how old you were?"

"Ohhh, at *least* five years old. Maybe five and a half."

"That old, huh?"

In a move so quick, she didn't see it coming, he reached for her and pulled her down so that she was sprawled on top of him. "I say, why tamper with something that works."

"Jarrod." His name, meant to be a protest, sounded breathless even to her.

"Stay here, just for a little while, Gena. I've missed you so much." One hand slipped beneath her T-shirt to her back, holding her firmly to him. The other hand went to her hair. He gathered the thickness of it into his hands and brought it around her head to lay it along one shoulder, so that her face was free of the golden strands. "I've missed being with you like this. Do you remember how we used to be?"

"I remember."

It must have been the tone of her voice that made him say, very gently, "Remember the good times, Gena, not the bad."

"That's the problem. There weren't any bad times, not really . . . not until . . . ."

"Don't!" His hand pressed urgently against her back. "Put out of your mind whatever you were about to remember. Just think how I used to hold you like this, sometimes all night." His arms were completely around her, one beneath her T-shirt, the other resting on her lower back, his hand on the spot where her bottom began to curve.

"Just remember how I used to touch you." His hands began to massage her skin, both under and over her clothes.

"And just remember how I used to kiss you."

The sensuality of it all was too much for Gena.

Of their own accord, her lips lowered to press against his. Lightly at first, with her mouth open only partially, she kissed him. She did no remembering; rather, she reacquainted herself with the rough velvet texture of his lips, her lips brushing back and forth, opening ever wider, until—it just happened—her tongue darted into the waiting warm cavern of his mouth, then again and again, finding at last what she was seeking. She shuddered at the impact of the meeting of their tongues.

He comforted her, rubbing his hand over her skin until her nerves were still again. But her blood surged, carrying sweet desire to every part of her.

Her torso lay over him, her legs between his. Momentarily she wished that she weren't wearing her jeans, so she could rediscover the warmth of his hair-roughened legs against hers. But even with the pants on, the length and hardness of him was apparent against that point where the denim legs of her jeans joined.

She placed her hands against the bed on either-side of his head, and tried to push up. "Jarrod, we're going to hurt you."

"It's okay," he murmured, pulling her back against him. He slid a hand over her spine and under one of her arms to her breast. His fingertips moved back and forth along her sensitive skin.

Her nipples tightened, and Gena knew he could feel them through the soft cotton of her shirt. "I want to stop, Jarrod . . . before we can't."

"That's quite an admission," he murmured as his fingers burrowed between their two bodies to close around the aching nub of her breast.

"What?" she asked, confused, her mind on what his fingers were doing to her nipple.

"That you might not be able to stop yourself from making love to me. Do you realize how far we've come from that first day, when I moved in?"

"Stop it, Jarrod!" She pushed his hand away, but, unable to find the strength to move off him she simply lowered her head to his shoulder and tried to regain her equilibrium. It was difficult, though. Their two hearts were beating with the same rapid rhythm. She could feel the heat of his skin against her cheek. She could almost taste him. No, she corrected herself, she *could* taste him. The flavor of him was still on her tongue, in her mouth.

With the pain of the inner agony of wanting him, she groaned and rolled off.

He turned on his side to face her. "It's okay, babe. I know you're not ready yet. But it's a start."

"I'd better leave," she said, not moving.

"I wish you wouldn't. Just stay. We won't do anything except be close." He smiled. "I want to be close to you, Gena."

Did she dare let herself get close to him again? Gena asked herself. He wasn't just talking about a physical relationship now, and that was scary.

"My jaw really does hurt," he whispered.

She broke into a laugh. "That's blackmail, Jarrod."

"You wouldn't be giving in," he said more seriously, "you would just be taking a small step toward something I think you want as much as I do."

When she said nothing, he continued. "We can have it all, babe."

She knew that he meant they could be friends as well as lovers, and she had to question whether it could really happen . . . even as she settled down to spend the night in his bed.

Six

The next day Donny Joe appeared with an aching head and a forlorn look on his face. He begged Rose to forgive him, and of course she did. After all, as Rose said herself, she loved men too much to stay mad at any one of them for long.

On Sunday, the only day Clancey's was closed, the residents of the boarding house, along with Donny Joe and two other men who were currently dangling after Rose, went to Fort Worth. They visited the stockyards, and that night they danced for hours at Billy Bob's, the famous country-and-western nightclub.

Gena and Jarrod spent every spare moment together. Over the next few days they did things that they had never taken the time for before. They went on a picnic, saw a movie, went sight-seeing, spent moments just gazing at each other.

They were wonderful days, Gena concluded, because it seemed as though what Jarrod had said was coming true. They were growing closer in every way. But at the same time, as the emotional distance between them lessened, her guilt over her illegal activities grew. Even though she had taken no further funds since the withdrawal for Peter's mother's car, it still weighed heavily on her mind. Her illegal acts stood between them, and she knew that soon she would have to find the courage to tell him what she had done.

"I want to go shopping," Jarrod announced one afternoon.

They were sitting in the parlor, working a jigsaw puzzle together. The puzzle depicted two kittens tangled up in a ball of twine, and trying to fit the pieces into the right spaces was driving Gena crazy.

"I can't go anywhere. I'm due at work in an hour. You know that."

"No, you aren't." Jarrod smiled. "Clancey gave you the afternoon off."

Gena gazed at him in amazement. "How did you manage that?"

He reached over and took a puzzle piece out of her hand, fitting it into the precise spot from which it had been cut. "Well, actually, I didn't. I had Rose ask him for me."

Gena grinned. "That was underhanded. You've

seen for yourself how flustered he gets around her. He'll agree to anything she says."

"The power of a woman."

"The power of *Rose*, you mean."

"The power you have over me is probably only somewhat less than that of a nuclear explosion."

She looked up from the corner of the puzzle she had been working on for the last twenty minutes. His voice had been light, but his brown eyes held a depth of seriousness that stirred something inside her. She swallowed. "So why do you want to go shopping?"

"I want to buy you a pretty dress. I've seen you in jeans for so long, I've forgotten what you look like in a dress. Not that I'm complaining." He smiled, and the effect of it curled in her stomach. "I believe I told you what you do to me when you bend over in those jeans." He fitted a piece of the puzzle into her corner of the puzzle with irritating accuracy.

"I won't let you buy me a dress, Jarrod."

"Please," he said with a sweetness that was entirely new to her. "I really want to, and I'll let you buy me something."

She eyed him suspiciously. "What?"

"I don't know. There are any number of things I need. Let's just go see what the good merchants of Dallas are selling today."

She chuckled. "I can guarantee that the good merchants of Dallas will sell you anything you want to buy. It's the way things are done in this town."

"That's what I like to hear. Capitalism running like a well-oiled machine."

They didn't have to drive far before they found a store that interested Jarrod. That it was a five and dime didn't seem to bother him.

"Come on, tell me the truth, Jarrod. Have you ever been in a five and dime store in you life?"

"Of course, many times . . . when I was a kid."

"Really? Well, okay"—she glanced around the store—"where shall we start?"

"This aisle looks like a good place." He grabbed her hand with enthusiasm. "Come on, I think I see the model-airplane section. Will you buy me a model airplane, Gena? Please?"

She did. She bought him a plastic model-airplane kit for three dollars and forty-nine cents, she bought him a bag of bubble gum for fifty cents, she bought him a Garfield pencil holder for a dollar ninety-nine, and a package of pencils imprinted with cartoon characters for ninety-eight cents. Finally, for four dollars and fifty-four cents she bought him a lampshade to cover his trout-shaped lamp. And she had never seen him look happier.

By the time they left the store, Gena's skepticism over Jarrod's idea had melted, and she had entered into their adventure with eagerness. When he spied an exclusive boutique that he said they must investigate, she barely demurred, even when she discovered the shop had carpet so thick you practically had to wade through it, and a glittering chandelier that swayed majestically from the ceiling.

The sleekly groomed saleswoman greeted them with a welcoming smile that slipped a little when she saw Gena's jeans and T-shirt. "Good afternoon. My name is Myrna. What can I help you with today?"

"We're just looking," Gena said.

"Not really," Jarrod corrected. "I would like to buy a very special dress for my fiancée."

Gena frowned at him, but the saleswoman beamed. "Fiancée, how very nice. Congratulations!"

Jarrod saw Myrna cast a discreet glance at Gena's ringless left hand. He reached for his billfold, unfolded it, produced a Platinum American Express Card, and handed it to her. "If we go over the standard credit line, I'll pay cash. Will that be all right?"

Myrna almost fainted. "Why, certainly, sir. If you'll just come this way, we have a very comfortable chair you can sit in while I help your beautiful fiancée find just the right dress."

"Good, very good," he murmured, tossing a conspiratorial glance at Gena and following Myrna. "And perhaps I could have a glass of white wine?"

"Right away, sir." Myrna snapped her fingers and a young assistant appeared. "A glass of white wine right away for Mr. Saxon, and one for his fiancée also." The young girl nodded and hurried away.

Gena should have been mad, but she couldn't seem to work up the energy. Jarrod was having too good a time. Besides, it had been nearly a year since she had been in a dress store as nice as this one, and she was feminine enough to want to try on some of the beautiful clothes surrounding her.

Once Jarrod was made comfortable, Myrna ushered Gena into a dressing room decorated in soft hues of peach and blue. Then Myrna and her assistant began to bring in a variety of garments.

Jarrod leaned back in the chair and took sips of the wine, his eyes trained on the dressing-room door. At last it opened and Gena came out, swathed in a length of multi-hued pink chiffon. She stopped in front of the mirror and regarded herself. The strapless bodice fit tightly, pushing her breasts into creamy mounds that swelled over the low top.

"What do you think, Jarrod? Do you like this?"

How could he tell her that she took his breath away? he wondered. "It's very nice."

She tilted her head, looking at herself from another angle. "Yes, it is, isn't it? Too bad I have no place to wear it."

Come home with me, to Philadelphia, where you'll have any number of places you can wear it, he wanted to say. But he said nothing.

Suddenly she laughed and gathered up a handful of the skirt in each hand, holding the fabric far out on either side. Then she twirled around and around, the image of a young girl in her first long dress. The pastel chiffon brushed against Jarrod's face, the touch of the filmy material sparking erotic sensations . . . and thoughts.

Happily Gena spun one last time, overbalanced, and fell in Jarrod's lap. His hands came up to catch her. Resting in his arms, she threw back her head and laughed. She was out of breath and her cheeks were flushed, and Jarrod wondered how he kept from grinding his mouth into hers and kissing her until they were both senseless.

Because she was positioned at an awkard angle, one breast threatened to overflow its bounds. Lord, but he wanted to hold her nakedness, to touch it, to taste it! He tore his gaze away from the sight, and their eyes met. For a split second, passion shimmered like flames between them. Involuntarily Jarrod's hand moved to her breast.

"Are you all right, miss?" the assistant asked.

Jarrod jerked his hand away.

"Yes, yes. Thank you," Gena murmured.

Next was a navy-blue mini-skirt. The saleswoman had chosen a periwinkle-blue silk shirt to go with it. Gena emerged from the dressing room barefoot and viewed herself in the mirror with a frown. "I don't know. There's something about this that doesn't look right. What do you think, Jarrod?"

He thought it was one of the sexiest outfits he had ever seen, but if her told her that, he would have to reveal that his loins were pulsing with a heat that was rapidly rising to the boiling point. "It's fine."

"I think you would be more pleased with the outfit miss, if you had the proper shoes," the assistant suggested. "I'll be right back."

Gena turned and smiled at Jarrod. "This is fun.

I'm glad you thought of it. Of course we're not going to buy anything."

"Of course not."

Through the silk of the blouse he could make out the full, round shape of her breasts, the pointed tips jutting temptingly. He wondered what she would taste like through the silk. He longed to draw both her flesh and the silk into his mouth, to find out.

"Here we are, miss." The young girl handed Gena a pair of high-heeled shoes with straps that buckled around the ankles.

Gena dropped the shoes onto the floor and stepped into them, then bent from the waist to buckle the straps. Her enchanting rear end presented itself to Jarrod, and he had to put down the wineglass because his hand was shaking so badly. The mini-skirt rose high up the backs of her legs, revealing a long, smooth expanse that, to his overheated imagination, seemed to go on forever. The skirt hugged her shapely bottom snugly. As badly as he had wanted her that night at Clancey's, when he had first seen her bending over in jeans, he wanted her twice as much now.

Damn! In a minute he was going to embarrass himself.

In the next half hour Gena paraded before him in various outfits, and surprisingly, each was more modest than the last. But his desire only increased. Absorbed in the clothes she was trying on, Gena turned this way and that before him, pulling and tugging at the garments, adjusting them so that they draped just so over her body, until Jarrod thought he would lose his mind.

At last she came out in a demure amber silk shirtwaist with a full, swirling skirt. "We'll take that one," he barked.

"Jarrod, I don't want you to buy anything for me!"

"We aren't going to talk about it," he muttered, his teeth clenched tightly. His gaze slashed to the hovering saleswoman. "Ring it up."

Gena cast him a bewildered look, and went to change. Jarrod was able to sit still for approximately thirty seconds. Then he bolted upright and headed after Gena.

He flung the door of the dressing room open, then stopped. Gena, with the dress unbuttoned and pulled half off one shoulder, turned in surprise.

Slowly he entered and closed the door behind him.

"Jarrod, you shouldn't be in here!"

"Really?" Two steps brought him within inches of her. "Who made that rule?" He dropped a kiss on her exposed shoulder.

"Probably that saleswoman out there. I can only imagine what she's thinking."

He stripped down the other side of the amber silk garment until the bodice bunched around Gena's waist. Her breasts were exposed to his hungry gaze, but he didn't touch her. He only looked, and as he did, he could feel the perspiration bead his upper lip. Her breasts rose high and firm, perfect, with taut nipples that drove a man to pull them into his mouth. . . .

Jarrod did. He bent and drew a nipple to his lips with a control that heightened and magnified his need. He suckled first one breast and then the other. Only when Gena's moans grew too loud for the small dressing room did he stop.

"I don't care what Myrna is thinking, and rules are made to be broken," he murmured. "She has my Platinum American Express Card with a twenty-five-thousand-dollar credit line. She wouldn't object if I hung from the chandelier nude."

"I'm sure you're right." Gena's breathless voice quickened his inflamed blood until it was pounding. "In fact it would probably make her day."

"How about your day?" He kissed her other shoulder.

She looked up at him, helpless in her desire. "Mine too."

His mouth lowered until it was a breath away from hers. "If I don't do this, I'll go crazy."

And then he kissed her. It was a complete kiss and one that Gena felt in every cell of her body. This was madness, she thought. They couldn't make love in this dressing room! Not with that saleswoman just outside.

But his mouth was so sure, so urgent on her own. And his hands brushed her skin with such heat. . . .

Then she heard Jarrod echo her thoughts. "I can't make love to you here, but Lord, I wish I had you back at the house!"

"No . . . no." She felt compelled to object, but at the same time wondered why. "I have to work tonight."

Jarrod pulled away, his eyes glittering feverishly. "It doesn't matter, Gena. I will have you, soon . . . soon."

The bar was packed to overflowing. To Gena everything seemed to be in excess—the customers seemed more demanding, Clancey more agitated, even Rose to be flirting more than average. What was it about tonight, she asked herself, that made her feel as though she were atop a volcano about to erupt?

Jarrod was at his accustomed table. Was her imagination working overtime, Gena wondered, or was he watching her more closely than usual?

Cole Garrett had come in a few minutes earlier, but instead of requesting a table, he had taken a seat at the bar. Looking more perfectly put together than ever, he, too, was watching her. No, she decided, giving herself a good mental shake, it was just a bad case of nerves. The afternoon's shopping expedition had stirred up passionate feelings that now must be suppressed, again. . . .

She passed Cole on her way to the kitchen to turn in an order, but she didn't acknowledge him by so much as a look. She didn't feel capable of polite conversation. But she wasn't overly surprised when he spoke as she was emerging from the kitchen. "Gena, how is Sugar this evening?"

He could not have said anything better calculated to bring her to a stop. And by the gleam in his eye, he knew it.

"Sugar? She's just fine."

"Good, good. She's certainly deserves to spend her declining years in peace."

"Declining years?" Now he really had Gena's attention. "What in the hell are you talking about?"

The big, redheaded bartender responded to her tone of voice and stepped over. "Is everything all right, Gena?"

Gena didn't take her eyes off Cole. "I'm not sure, Jake, but I'll let you know."

"I'll be close. Just call."

Cole smiled. "He's quite protective, isn't he? But then, I can understand that." He ran the back of his hand down her cheek. "You're very beautiful. I'm sure I'm just one of many men who want you. However, Gena, I think you should know that I'll be the one to get you."

He had never been quite so blunt before, though Gena had known he desired her. Before tonight she hadn't really thought him the type to make a blatant pass. In the time it took her to blink she quickly reassessed Cole Garrett. She had known he was dangerous. Now she realized that he felt he held some trump card over her, and she knew that it had to do with Sugar.

She rested one arm on the bar and leaned closer to prevent anyone from overhearing their conversation. "What are you holding over Sugar? Tell me, Cole, I want to know."

"I thought you would." He tilted his head toward her, bringing them even closer. "What is that wonderful fragrance you wear? Whatever it is, I'll buy you a gallon of it."

"If you think I'm going to beg you—"

"I love that image—you, begging me."

"—then you're very wrong. I can get it out of Sugar, and you know I can. So either tell me or this conversation is at an end."

Clancey danced by, alarm making his movements jerky. "Gena, you have orders waiting in the kitchen! Hurry! Hurry!"

Cole reached into his jacket and took out one of his business cards. He flipped it over and quickly scrawled an address on the back. "If Sugar hasn't told you yet, then she's not going to. Come to my house tonight after you leave work. I'll have a late supper waiting. We'll talk then."

Gena took the card and, with a glance at the address, shoved it into her jeans pocket. She had grave reservations about going to his house alone. Still, although she had told him she could get the information out of Sugar, she wasn't so sure she could. To get Sugar to confide in her would be far from easy. Whatever was happening between Sugar and Cole, the older woman seemed to have decided to ignore it.

"Well?"

Gena looked up and found Cole's cold gray eyes on her. "I'll be there."

"Good." He tilted his bourbon glass toward her in a mock toast. "I'll look forward to seeing you."

With that he threw some money on the bar, and walked away.

Gena stared at Cole's retreating back. And as she did, her gaze collided with Jarrod's. That he was furious was obvious. She had forgotten that he would have seen the whole encounter with Cole! Well, there was nothing she could do to help it, she decided. He would just have to understand.

"Gena, Gena!" Clancey was practically standing on his head, he was so upset.

Rose sashayed up to her boss. "Clancey, have I ever told you that I just love a man who gets excited?" To Gena she murmured, "I suppose you've noticed that Handsome practically has steam coming out of his ears."

"I'm afraid I have."

"Anything I can do?"

"I don't know. I haven't figured out how to handle it yet."

"I saw you talking to Cole, and I have to tell you—"

"I know what you're going to say, believe me. The warning isn't necessary."

"Ladies, ladies, our customers are waiting! *Waiting*!"

Rose turned a beaming smile on Clancey and planted a big kiss square on his mouth. "Clancey, you're such a turn-on!"

Gena went to pick up her orders, idly thinking that she might have to do CPR on Clancy before the night was over.

Her earlier impression that she was sitting on a

simmering volcano proved to be correct. The next time she walked by Jarrod's table he grabbed her arm. "Sit down."

"I can't, you know that. I'm working."

"Sit down, Gena!"

Gena felt the stares of several customers seated at surrounding tables. "All right," she whispered, "just for a minute, but don't make a scene."

Jarrod leaned across the table, and she saw that his mouth had gone white with anger. "I can't be responsible for what I'll do next unless you tell me exactly what you were doing with that man at the bar."

"Nothing! I was just talking to him." Since she had been in Dallas, she had not had to account to anyone for her time or her actions, and Jarrod's display of possessiveness grated slightly. Yet at the same time his obvious jealousy generated a stirring warmth in her heart. What was happening to her?

"You talked to him far too long for it to have been a casual conversation."

Gena looked at Jarrod in amazement. "I've never seen you like this before."

"I'll admit that I don't think I experienced a jealous moment before you ran away." He was talking as softly as he could, but his words carried a great intensity. "I don't like it, I'm not particularly proud of it, but there it is. Now are you going to tell me?"

She nodded. "Yes, I will, and I want you to give me your word that you'll try to understand."

He sat back in his chair. "I haven't even heard what you're about to say and already I don't like it."

"Just listen to me. The man I was talking to is Cole Garrett. He owns a local real-estate-development firm. He's asked me to go to his house tonight after work, and I'm going."

"No, you're not."

"Jarrod—"

"*No*, you are not!" he said more loudly.

She raised a warning finger to her lips. "I have to. He has some information I want, and—"

"You have something he wants. Just how dumb do you think I am, Gena?"

She rubbed her forehead. "Look, Jarrod, it concerns Sugar."

"I don't care who the hell it concerns! I don't want you within ten feet of that man, much less in his house."

Suddenly Gena had to fight a strong urge to laugh at him. He was being so adamant . . . so obstinate . . . and so very dear! He was reacting, she realized, like a typical man, a man who was head over heels in love with a woman. . . . Then the full impact hit her of what she had just thought. *He really did love her.* She had no idea why it had taken this show of rabid jealousy finally to convince her of his love, when she knew all too well just how much he had sacrificed to live in Dallas and be with her. But like a flash it came to her: He really did love her!

The problem was, now that she was convinced,

she wasn't sure she was ready to face her own feelings. There was just too much involved, and she had a lot to think through. Besides, before she made any decision, she had to find out if Sugar was in trouble. . . .

She reached over and took his hand. "Jarrod, just go back to the boarding house, will you? When I get home we'll talk about it."

"I'm staying right here until you're off. And then I'm driving you home."

Gena stifled a sigh, wondering what she was going to do now.

Rose sidled by. "Don't look now, but Clancey is about to come apart at the seams. It should be an interesting show."

"How long until closing?" Gena asked her.

"An hour, but I say let's close up now. We could go honky-tonkin'. I feel like shaking my bootie. What do you think, Handsome? Want to come?"

"An excellent idea," Jarrod said.

"No! No! I'll be ruined!" Clancey hurried over to Jarrod's table, having overheard the last snatch of conversation. They all watched, fascinated, as the half-Chinese, half-Irish man began to take on the look of a full-blooded Indian, circling the table, doing a remarkable imitation of a war dance, and chanting, "The customers, the customers, oh, my God, the customers!"

Rose leaned over to Gena and Jarrod. "I think we've finally pushed Clancey to his limit, poor man. It's definitely time I did something about him. Fortunately I've got a secret weapon in reserve."

As Clancey completed his fourth or fifth circle around the table—Gena wasn't sure which; she had lost count—Rose grabbed his arm and, talking softly in his ear, led him off toward the kitchen.

"I wonder what she means by secret weapon?" Gena said, watching them go.

"Knowing Rose, there's no telling," Jarrod answered. "But whatever it is, nothing has changed. I'll be waiting for you when you get off work."

Gena glared at him. His possessiveness was becoming wearing, especially now that it was interfering with something she needed to do. "You're being ridiculous, Jarrod. Going to Cole's tonight has nothing to do with you and me. I told you. It's about Sugar."

He crossed his arms over his chest and returned her glare. "Then we'll take care of it tomorrow, *together.* But tonight you're going home with me."

Furious, she jerked up from the table.

"Waitress?" Jarrod called. "Could you bring me a piece of pie and a cup of coffee, please?"

Gena smiled sweetly. "Certainly, sir. I'll bring it right away."

She made the rounds of her tables, checking to make sure her customers had everything they needed. She even delivered Jarrod's coffee and pie without succumbing to the urge to dump them in his lap. Then she headed for the kitchen. There she found Clancey and Rose. Clancey was sitting in one corner, staring at nothing in particular.

Rose was chatting with the cook, waiting for an order. When Gena walked in, Rose swung around. "Is everything all right?"

"No. Far from it." She glanced at Clancey. "Is he okay?"

"Don't worry. I've got him under control. I guarantee that within a week he'll be a new man."

"Then you're a certified worker of miracles."

"Absolutely. Now, can I do anything for you?"

"No, thanks. It's something I've got to take care of myself. I need to go to Cole Garrett's after work, and Jarrod is saying he won't let me. Get that! *He* won't let me."

"Well, I don't mean to be butting in where I shouldn't"—Rose paused to think over what she had just said, then flashed Gena an irrepressible, dimpled smile—"but then, why the hell not? Listen, kid. A man like Handsome, out there, doesn't come along every day. If I were you I'd tell Cole Garrett to stuff himself up the tailpipe of his Mercedes and then I'd go home with Jarrod."

Gena groaned. "You don't understand. I'm not going to Cole's because I want to. I'm going because I've got to find out what he's doing to Sugar. Something's going on there."

Rose had thrown an idle glance in Clancey's direction, but Gena's words brought her platinum-blond head whipping around. "Sugar? Cole's giving Sugar trouble?"

"I think so. I've tried to get it out of her, but she won't tell me anything. He said if I came over tonight, he'd tell me what's going on."

Rose's black eyes took on a mischievous sparkle. "You know, Cole may be a snake in many ways, but he's also a man, and I can melt the starch out of his shorts any day of the week."

"What in the world are you talking about?"

"I'm talking about your going home with Handsome and my taking your palce at Cole's."

"No, no." Gena rejected the idea with a shake of her head. "I couldn't let you do that. Besides, Jarrod has a thing or two to learn, if he thinks he can order me around."

Rose shrugged, conveying that she thought Gena had made the wrong choice. "Okay, but if you change your mind, the offer stands."

At closing time Gena and Rose left together. Jarrod was waiting for them out on the sidewalk. Without saying a word he took Gena's arm and began steering her toward his car.

Her anger at this action made her forget that just an hour before, she had finally become convinced of his love for her. Peevishly she jerked her arm away. "Excuse me, but I'm not going anywhere with you."

"Yes, you are," he said calmly, opening his car door and stuffing her inside. "Rose, do you want a ride?"

"Thanks, but I've got someplace else to go. Right, Gena?" She leaned down, rested her forearm along the door window, and held out her other hand. Resignedly Gena reached in her pocket for Cole's card. "Thanks, Rose. And good luck."

*   *   *

The short drive to Sugar's was silent, and that was just as Gena wanted it. She sat in the corner of the front seat, trying to sort through her feelings, but her thoughts were in confusion.

Perhaps she could let go of the hurt and anger that had been weighing heavily on her ever since that day when she had sat in the lawyer's office to hear her father's will read. She was no longer convinced it really mattered that Jarrod owned Alexander's. Although she had enjoyed working with the Alexander's computers, it was not as if she'd had any aspiration to run the company itself. She had never discussed this with her father, yet perhaps he had known how she felt.

But, and it was a large *but*, she supposed it was the principle of the thing that still concerned her. The company should rightfully belong to her.

And then she almost groaned aloud, because it was all so complicated.

Yet . . . perhaps, at last, after all these months, she could allow herself to admit that she did love Jarrod, had in fact never stopped loving him.

Perhaps.

But if she and Jarrod were to have any chance at all for a life together, she was going to have to tell him the complete truth about the Sherwood Preservation Society. Tell him before he found out for himself.

Would he understand? Gena asked herself, watching the street lights blend into one continuous streak of light as the car zoomed along. Would he forgive her? By now she had taken well over a hundred thousand dollars from Alexander's. That would require a lot of forgiveness and understanding, by anyone's standards.

The problem was, she didn't feel she really knew him well enough to gauge what his reaction would be. Instinctively she felt that he was still keeping a portion of himself from her. And even if he did forgive her and come to understand why she had embezzled the money, there was another problem. Sooner or later he would want her to go back to Philadelphia with him, resume her old life, while he guided his two companies straight to the top of the business world.

And she wasn't ready for that. She was much too afraid. For if they went back now, might not things between herself and Jarrod return to the way they had been? And Gena couldn't stand that. Back home, they had been lovers. Here their relationship was deepening. They were becoming friends.

Gena's jumbled thoughts kept her busy during the drive, but as soon as the car stopped, she leaped out and rushed up the steps to the front door. She was halfway to the second-floor landing before Jarrod entered the house. "Gena, wait!"

She continued on up the stairs, taking them two at a time. Sure that at any moment she would feel Jarrod's footsteps close behind her, she was glad when she heard Sugar call out to detain him.

He had acted like a first-class jerk tonight, Jarrod

thought with disgust. But dammit! When he watched Garrett touch her, he had nearly torn Clancey's place apart.

Maybe it would have been better if he had, he told himself. At least then he would have vented his frustrations on Garrett—and Clanccy's furniture—rather than on Gena.

Instead he had exercised his powers of restraint to their breaking point. He had even congratulated himself on being successful. And then he had proceeded to alienate Gena even further. What a bloody fool he was! Now he was very much afraid he had ruined whatever progress he had managed to make with her.

Jarrod paced the bare floor of his room, trying to decide what to do. He had overcome many obstacles in his life—after his father's death, he'd had to—but he had never faced a challenge that equaled that of winning Gena back. And he had never faced one that meant as much to him. He wasn't going to give up. He loved her more than ever now.

He would think of something. He had to.

As she sat on the window seat in her room, gazing out at the night, Gena pulled the hand-crocheted shawl closer around her. Beneath the shawl she had on only the thin white cotton nightgown she had worn all summer. But the nights were growing colder now, and since the delicately embroidered gown provided no more covering or warmth than the lightest or barest of slips, she was grateful for the shawl, which had been a gift from Sugar.

The gown had been a gift from Rose, embroidered by her before the start of summer. A smile curved Gena's lips as she remembered her surprise when Rose had given her the gown. She would never have believed Rose to have the desire or the patience to do such exquisite needlework. Gena's smile gentled at the thought that her friend Rose was the most unexpected person she had ever known.

In a way, she supposed her father's will had been a blessing. It had provided the circumstances that had allowed her to meet all the wonderful people here in Dallas—Rose, Sugar, Bertrand, Clancey, Peter, Bobby. The list was a long and amazing one.

But perhaps most amazing of all was that Jarrod was part of that list now too. She had underestimated both his patience and his desire.

One day he was completely out of her life; the next day he was an integral part of it. Her friends had accepted him without question. Rose flirted with him, Sugar depended on him for repairs around the house, and Bertrand loved to share complaints, both imaginary and real, with him.

But what about Gena?

When the knock on the door came a little while later, Gena remained quiet—she didn't want to talk to anyone else tonight—but the knock sounded again, then again, until it finally dawned on her that this could be Rose, already back from Cole's.

She slipped off the window seat and went to answer the door. Instead of Rose, however, she found Jarrod.

He was leaning against the doorjamb, his hands behind his back. Her throat went dry at the sight of him. He had changed from the slacks and sweater he'd had on at Clancey's into a burgundy velour robe that stopped at mid-thigh. Because his hands were behind his back, the lapels of his robe were drawn back, revealing his broad chest. Beads of water from a recent shower clung to the fine brown hair on his chest. Through the opening of his robe, she could even make out a flat brown nipple.

Need, with all its emotional and physical connotations, came to her, quick and jarring as a thunderclap.

"May I come in?" Jarrod asked quietly. "I brought you a peace offering."

So caught up was she with his physical presence, it didn't occur to Gena to answer him.

Jarrod didn't appear to notice. Taking her silence for acquiescence, he moved into the room. With a well-placed foot he shut the door behind him. His gaze slid over the femininity of her gown and the way her shining golden hair spilled over her shoulders and down her back.

Without bringing his hands from behind his back, he leaned toward her and placed a light kiss on her lips. When he raised his head, he whispered, "You're the most beautiful woman I've ever known."

He smelled clean and soapy, as well as very male. "Thank you . . . very much." She swallowed hard. "You said you brought a peace offering?"

He drew his hands from behind his back. In one he held a half gallon of cookies-and-cream ice cream. In the other he held a spoon.

"You brought only one spoon," she said, then cringed, because it seemed to her that she had never made a stupider remark.

"We've always used just one spoon," he pointed out, glancing around the room. "I thought we could share, like always. Where were you sitting?"

"Uh . . . oh . . . the window seat."

"That doesn't look wide enough for both of us. Frankly neither does the love seat. I guess that leaves the bed."

"I don't think—"

He stopped what she was about to say with an impatient lift of his eyebrow. "We're just going to sit on the bed. If anything else happens, it will be up to you."

She supposed she was being silly, yet somehow his words didn't reassure her. But he was already arranging his long frame on her bed. Drawn to him despite herself, she crossed the room to the bed. Instead of sitting back against the pillows and headboard as Jarrod was, however, she chose a spot to the side of him, level with his knee, and faced him. As an old etiquette book might have instructed, she kept one foot planted carefully on the floor.

Her stomach felt tied in knots—knots of fear because of what could happen between them, and knots of excitement for the same reason. The reenactment of this old ritual between them seemed, under their present circumstances, to be entirely too intimate. As had their activities of this afternoon.

From the corner of her eye, she peered at Jarrod. If this familiarity was affecting him, he wasn't showing it. He dipped the spoon into the smooth surface of the ice cream, brought up a heaping portion, and, as had been their custom, offered the first bite to her.

"No, you go first," she murmured. *Anything* to break the cycle of how it once had been.

Jarrod looked at her thoughtfully, and suddenly stuck the spoon back in the ice cream. "You know what?"

"No, what?" Her attention had focused on his bathrobe, tied with an extremely loose knot. It looked to her as if the knot might come undone at any moment. And to make matters worse—or was it better?—when he had climbed on the bed, the short hem of the robe had crawled even higher up his thighs. Gena had forgotten how thick and hard with muscles his thighs were. She felt like a prim young girl, in bed—no, she corrected herself, *on* a bed—with a man for the first time. Her nerves were threatening to come unstrung, and she suddenly noticed that she was having trouble breathing.

His deep voice, close beside her, made her jump. "You're too far away. I want you closer."

With a startlingly easy movement, one that caught her completely off guard, he opened his legs and shifted her between them. Now she was sitting cross-legged, within the circle of his body. His robe had parted, baring his thighs all the way up. . . . Gena quickly looked away, but she knew he had followed her gaze. . . .

Slowly, casually, he readjusted his robe until it covered him properly. Then, with a satisfied smile, he leaned back. "Now, that's better. Are you sure you don't want to go first?"

Unfortunately for Gena's equilibrium, when Jarrod had leaned back, his robe had crept back up. "Positive."

"Okay." He slipped the spoon into his mouth, and when he retracted it, a small mound of ice cream remained. He held it out to her.

Gena took it, staring at the substance that had just been in Jarrod's mouth. Slowly she placed the spoon in her own. The cool ice cream touched her lips, her tongue, then slid down her throat to her stomach. Unfortunately, it did nothing to stop the warmth that was spreading rapidly through her insides.

Seven

As soon as she could she handed the spoon back to him. "What made you think of this?"

"What?" Another spoonful slipped into his mouth. "You mean, ask you to share the ice cream with me?" He swallowed, and dipped the spoon back into the container. Then, instead of handing her the spoon, he brought it to her lips and prodded gently with the tip until she opened her mouth. Slowly he fed her. A bit of a cookie slid onto her tongue, and she tasted its sweetness.

He smiled. "Good, huh? It's been a long time since we've done this, hasn't it, babe?"

She wished he wouldn't call her that! She wished he weren't half-naked. "You didn't answer me," she prodded.

"Ah, Gena," he said sadly. "Let me tell you something, all right?"

She nodded.

"I knew I had made a jerk out of myself tonight," Jarrod began. "I didn't know how to begin to apologize. So I . . ." Meeting her gaze, he lifted his shoulders and let them fall. "I'm sorry. I really didn't have any right to prevent you from going to Garrett's house. I acted the way I did tonight because I wish I *did* have a right but . . . I don't."

His admission touched her. She raised her hand to his cheek. "I told you. I was going to Cole's on Sugar's behalf, and not for any other reason."

He caught her hand and brought it to his mouth, kissing the delicate skin inside her wrist.

"I know. I guess I knew it earlier tonight, but reason is rarely operative when it comes to you." All at once he smiled. "There's some ice cream on your chin."

"Oh, I'll . . ."

He held her hand firm, preventing her from wiping her chin. Instead he leaned forward and, with his tongue, licked the ice cream away. "Remember when we used to dribble ice cream on each other on purpose?" he asked softly.

The darkening of her eyes told him she remembered.

What was the use? she asked herself.

She loved him with a power that overwhelmed her.

She wanted him so much, it seemed her blood constantly called to him.

"Jarrod . . . I'm so tired of fighting with you."

Slowly he released her hand. "What are you saying?"

"I'm tired of fighting my feelings for you."

He set aside the ice cream. With great care he slipped the shawl from her shoulders, but then he stopped. "You look very young and innocent in that gown. I almost feel I shouldn't touch you."

"Then I'll take it off." She spoke and acted at the same time. In an instant her gown was over her head and tossed to the far corner of the room.

A gasp escaped Jarrod's lips, and it was the single most beautifully erotic sound Gena had ever heard. All time, all space, all thought dissolved, until suddenly they were holding each other, kissing as though they had never stopped.

His robe had finally come open, so that Gena could experience the texture of his skin, which was both smooth and rough. She touched him; he touched her.

His hands seemed to be everywhere as they skimmed over her body, softly, lovingly; then they stopped to linger in secret places he remembered.

Her arms tightened around him; his came back to tighten around her. Then she was lying flat, with his warm weight on top of her. It felt so right, she was astonished that this hadn't happened before tonight. Now that she had conquered the stubborn pride that had kept them apart, she couldn't wait to be joined with him.

On fire, she begged, "Now."

"No, babe, not yet." His voice came out a ragged

gasp. "This is something I've wanted for so long, I must savor it."

He took her breast, filling his hand with her, pressing the soft flesh with his fingers so that the nipple pushed higher . . . closer . . . to his waiting lips.

As soon as his lips closed on its stiffened tip, Gena moaned. His mouth was cold from the ice cream, but it warmed quickly. "Oh, you're right. I want to savor it too. Make it last all night."

He gave a low laugh. "With a little food and a little rest in between, I can make it last for the rest of our lives." His mouth skimmed across her stomach, kissing her until her skin was glowing. Cupping her buttocks with his hands, he stopped raining kisses over her only to let his tongue circle her navel, then dip into the sweet recess.

"I must be dying," she murmured. "This is too much pleasure to bear."

She didn't so much hear his next words as feel them, vibrating against the inner petals of her womanhood. "This is living, babe. Accept the pleasure. Climb as high as you can."

She climbed . . . higher . . . and higher . . . until she was close to the peak.

Then he joined his body with hers and took her even higher.

She was warm, wrapped in a cloud, relaxed to the point where she wasn't even sure where her arms and legs were. Oh, she felt two arms and two legs. She just wasn't sure whose they were. Were they Jarrod's? Or was it his legs, her arms? Briefly she wondered how many combinations she could come up with, and decided it didn't matter.

She loved this weight-free, worry-free existence. It was even sound-free.

No . . . wait . . . there was sound. She listened. What was it that was trying to draw her back to earth? Who was it?

"The ice cream melted."

"What?"

"The ice cream melted all over your night table."

"What?"

"Wake up, babe."

In her sleep she smiled. Babe. The voice had called her babe. There was only one person in the world who called her babe, and that was Jarrod. The man she loved. The man who loved her.

His mouth covered hers, kissing her softly. Without raising his lips from hers, he asked. "Is this the same woman who wanted our lovemaking to last for the rest of our lives?"

"This is part of lovemaking," she said into his mouth, accepting his breath of life into her. "Coming out of a cloud to find that you're still holding me."

"And I'll never let you go again, either."

His tongue slipped as far into her mouth as it could reach. For Jarrod the sensation was like dipping into a jar of warm honey. . . .

Then, while Gena's eyes were still closed, he entered her, filling her as completely as he could.

It was his way of becoming a part of her. He hated the thought of having to draw out of her, even a little bit. He wanted to stay big and hard, inside her forever. . . .

He wanted to become an absolute necessity to her.

He wanted so much, but she began to move beneath him, and he couldn't help himself. . . .

Sometime later, Gena heard a sound that seemed to come from near her ear. Or what she thought was her ear. . . .

"That ice cream has made a hell of a mess."

"What?"

"The ice cream."

She wondered if she should open her eyes.

"Ah, ha! You're awake."

"How can you have so much energy?" she complained. "And what are you talking about?"

"Remember the ice cream?"

"Vaguely."

He laughed softly. "What *do* you remember?"

"You . . . me . . . clouds."

"I don't remember any clouds."

She put her arms around him and pulled him close. "Come with me. I'll show you."

When next she woke, the sun was shining into the room and she was alone in bed. She bolted straight up.

"Good morning."

Intense relief washed over her when she heard his voice. She turned to see Jarrod on the floor beside the bed, a rag in his hand.

"What *are* you doing?"

"I'm trying to scrub this table. It's all sticky. The ice cream got into the wicker."

"You'll never get it out that way! I'll take the table out in the yard and hose it down later."

"Won't your neighbors think that's a little strange?"

"A little strange? The people who live in *this* house? Are you kidding?"

"You've got a point."

"Come back to bed."

It was lunchtime before Gena and Jarrod made it out of her apartment. Jarrod took the table into the yard, but at Rose's call Gena detoured into the parlor.

Rose sat there alone, painting her nails a bright, electric red. Conspicuously, a pile of men's clothes lay in the center of the floor. A pile of expensive-looking men's clothes.

Gena eyed it curiously. The clothes looked remarkably like those Cole had worn the night before—right down to his shoes and socks.

"What's all this?"

A dimple flashed in Rose's cheek. "I challenged Cole to a game of strip Trivial Pursuit."

"You *didn't*!"

"I did. He was remarkably bad at the game."

"How bad?" Gena asked cautiously.

"I didn't have to remove so much as an eyelash." Camping it up, she batted her false eyelashes at Gena.

"Good going! So what did you find out?"

Rose lifted her shoulders, bewildered. "It seems that all he did was ask Sugar if she'd like to sell the house. Sugar said no. That's it. No big deal."

Gena sank into a chair, completely baffled. "How odd. I had the distinct impression that there was something heavier going on between them."

"Evidently not." Rose waved her hands through the air to dry her nails. "So was your evening successful?"

Gena stood up and walked to the window so that she could see Jarrod. "Very."

"Was that your night table I saw Handsome carrying downstairs?"

"Yeah. He's washing ice cream out of it."

"Ice cream, huh? Have you ever tried grapes?"

"Rose!"

"Try 'em. They're not nearly so messy."

Gena had to smile at her friend. "Sometimes I wonder if you're as bad as you let on."

Rose sent her a guileless look. "Bad? You mean *good*, don't you?"

The days that followed were some of the happiest Gena had ever known. Jarrod never once suggested that they return to Philadelphia. She knew that he still received packets of work every day via Express Mail, and that he worked on them while she was at Clancey's. But he never discussed this with her—nor did he mention Philadelphia.

Things were even going well at the bar. Clancey had become the "new man" Rose had promised. Her secret weapon turned out to be a petite, blue-eyed, redheaded, freckle-faced young waitress named Lotus Blossom. Lotus was half-Irish and half-Chinese, but looked Irish. Rose said she figured it was a match made in heaven, and Clancey seemed to agree. He no longer yelled at the help. He no longer cared whether his customers got waited on promptly or not. He no longer cared whether anyone ate venison. He just sat around all day, a smile on his face, and watched Lotus Blossom. . . .

Gena was happy for him, and she was happy for herself. With each passing day she became more relaxed, more confident of her relationship with Jarrod. The only thing that marred the perfection of the time spent together was Gena's secret—the Sherwood Preservation Society, and her alter ego, R. Hood. But she was afraid to tell Jarrod, so she put it off. There was little admirable in her delay, and she disliked herself for it. But guilt over her procrastination was insignificant compared to her fear of losing Jarrod. . . .

Soon, she promised herself. Soon she would tell him.

Gena shivered with pleasure as Jarrod's fingers worked between her legs, touching her in the exact spot, touching her in just the way that sent her senses spinning. She arched against the pressure of his hand, increasing the thrillingly hot sparks that coursed through her bloodstream with the quickness of electricity.

His mouth feasted at her breast. Her fingers tangled in his hair, holding him tightly against her. Complete ecstasy would soon be hers. She could feel the heat building. Jarrod wouldn't disappoint her. . . .

Sure enough he glided into her and began to take long, steady strokes, in, out, in. He reached deep inside her, discovering new spots to inflame, until that moment when a wash of rapture overtook her and she clung helplessly.

Sometime later she heard him murmur, "You know, I really like it here."

She raised her head and looked at him in mock astonishment. "Here, in my bed with me! You'd better!"

He pulled her head back to his shoulder. "Yes, here in your bed with you. But I was also talking about Sugar's boarding house. Remember the day we drove to White Rock Lake, and you told me that you loved it here because life was simple and the people were honest?"

"I remember." She had made that statement without considering that she herself was not honest. Now she felt like a hypocrite.

"Well, you were right. I've learned a lot, living here. Like the value of getting to know people who have nothing to do with my business; like the value of slowing down to enjoy life."

"When you first came I didn't believe you could take the slow pace."

"To tell you the truth, I wasn't sure I could either. But I was determined to win you back, and I would have made a pact with devil to do it."

"I'm not at all sure I'm worth it," Gena said quietly.

"You're worth it. And there's one more thing you should know. As soon as you're ready, I plan to sign over your father's company to you. It should have been yours to begin with. I never wanted it, and I certainly don't need it."

Her shock showed in her voice. "I'm not sure what to say."

"Don't say anything. Just think about it."

Perhaps he was right, she reflected. The issue of the ownership of Alexander's was best dropped for now. Wounds healed best when left alone.

She settled herself more comfortably against him. "Tell me what makes you tick. I want to know. Your drive to succeed has always amazed me, and I never could figure out what was behind it."

"A lot of pain was behind it."

"What do you mean?"

He paused and rearranged the covers over them. "I've never told you about my family."

"I assumed you didn't have one."

"I do, but the whole subject is hard for me to discuss. My mother is still alive. She lives in upstate New York, where I grew up."

Gena turned her head so she could see him. "Why didn't you ever take me to meet her, or at least tell me about her?"

"I don't see her much, I'm afraid, and I take total blame for our estrangement. Being here has given me a lot of time to think, however. And as soon as our lives are settled, you and I will pay her an extended visit. I've already called her a couple of times, and told her about you."

The proposed trip sounded wonderful to Gena, but she wasn't sure that Jarrod would want her to meet his mother after he heard what she had to tell him. "When did your father die?"

"He committed suicide when I was fourteen."

"Oh, Jarrod, how awful."

"Yes, it was. It completely devastated me. My father and I were very close. He was a good man, and he didn't deserve what happened to him."

"What do you mean?"

"Dad was a design engineer, quite brilliant in his way. He loved design; he taught me to love it too. Every Saturday he'd take me to the plant with him. I'd follow him around like a shadow. I remember being terribly proud of him." He looked down at her and brushed a strand of hair away from her face. "I still am. He was a wonderful father."

"He would have been proud of the way you turned out."

"I'm not so sure. I haven't always been a nice person. But then, I was driven to get revenge."

"Tell me."

"Dad had absolutely no business acumen. His partner, Ralph, handled the business end of the company. One day I got sick in school and was sent home. I remember riding my bicycle into the driveway. The garage door was closed, so I hopped off my bike, laid it down, and went to open the door. That's when I heard the car. I lifted the door, and a cloud of exhaust billowed out. I rushed in and flung the car door open . . . and there was my dad . . . unconscious. I dragged him out onto the driveway, talking to him all the while. I forget what I said. God, I was scared! I guess our next-door neighbor heard me because she came running out. I remember how she began to scream, and I yelled at her to call an ambulance. She did, and they came and took my dad to the hospital. It was too late, though."

Her heart went out to the little boy he had been and the man he was today. She wanted to hold him especially close so that nothing or no one would ever hurt him again. "Jarrod, I'm so sorry. Why haven't you ever told me this?"

"I've never told anyone. It hurt too much. And I guess I never felt secure enough with you before. I suppose the real truth is, I never trusted you enough."

"But now you do?"

"Yes."

She closed her eyes, sad because she didn't deserve his trust. She had a sudden wish to disappear from the face of the earth. . . .

"It wasn't until after the funeral that I learned

the reason for Dad's suicide. Without Dad's knowing it, his partner had been embezzling money from the company for years. Then, two days before payroll was due, Ralph skipped the country, taking every cent and leaving my dad to face a monumental debt alone. Dad couldn't handle it. He was like your dad, in that certain realities eluded him. He was—well—impractical. I suppose it was one of the reasons I was so fond of your father. He reminded me of mine. Your dad became a sort of father substitute for me."

Gena felt sick to the pit of her stomach. She couldn't say anything. All she could do was listen.

"Mom had to declare bankruptcy. She sold everything. In the end we moved in with her sister. Mom and I withdrew from each other, both grieving in our own ways.

"My world changed from that point on. I drove myself, first to make good grades in order to get a scholarship. Then, in college, I drove myself to excel, making sure I received an equally good foundation in both business and design. After college I established my own company, starting small, but growing gradually until I had rebuilt all that Dad had lost, and then exceeded it. But still it wasn't enough for me.

"Over the years I had made it my business to keep track of Ralph. At first he was in South America and I couldn't touch him. But five years ago he did something incredibly stupid, and it gave me an avenue for revenge. He changed his name and returned to this country. I nailed him. He'll be behind bars for a long time."

The coldness in Jarrod's voice turned Gena's heart to ice.

"My dad had trusted him, but Ralph betrayed him." Jarrod's voice trailed off, and he was silent for a minute. When he spoke again she could tell he was deliberately trying to force a lighter tone. "So now you know why I prize honesty so much. And why I'm so adamant that no one be allowed to take what is mine."

Trust, Gena thought. It all came down to that!

Her father hadn't trusted her enough to leave the company to her.

She hadn't trusted Jarrod and his love for her enough to stay after the reading of the will to hear his side.

And now Jarrod had just told her that he trusted her enough to tell her about his father's suicide, something that was obviously still very painful for him.

But he shouldn't trust her! She had betrayed him.

Eight

Thanksgiving day dawned sunny and cold. Inside Sugar's house there was great excitement. A fire blazed cheerily in the parlor, where several tables had been pushed together to form a single long one. Gena and Rose had laid tablecloths, and Sugar had put out her finest silver and china. Bertrand had taken on the centerpiece as his own special project, and had come up with a splendid arrangement of candles surrounded by Indian corn, gourds, and miniature pumpkins.

The residents of the boarding house eagerly awaited their guests, upon whose arrival there was much oh-ing and ah-ing.

Each guest brought a dish as a contribution to the dinner. As expected, Clancey had brought barbequed venison, but no one really minded, since

Jarrod had smoked two turkeys in a newly purchased smoker. To complement the turkeys Gena made several dishes of dressing, and to please Jarrod she wore the amber silk dress he had bought for her.

Sugar outdid herself by making a giant orange Jell-O salad that contained pineapple, whipped cream, and pecans. She had also made a large dish of sweet potatoes, soaked in a bourbon sauce and covered with a crunchy crust.

Bobby's family brought apple and pumpkin pies. Gena had to stare at the crusts for a long moment before she realized that what looked like lumps with sprouting wings were actually Bobby's attempt at dough apples.

Peter, his mother, and sister brought a wonderful vegetable casserole. It was the first time Gena had met Peter's mother, and the pride in the older woman's voice as she told Gena about her new job made Gena's eyes fill with tears of happiness.

Once again Rose surprised Gena, producing a row of perfectly baked loaves of bread. And she had actually donned something other than jeans and a T-shirt for the occasion: a dress made of a clingy fabric, with a surplice bodice that showed Rose's cleavage to its best advantage. To accent this chic ensemble, she had pinned a button to the dress. "Some of my best friends are turkeys," it announced.

Bertrand, unaware that Bobby's family would be bringing pies, had prepared a beautiful English trifle made up of luscious layers of ladyfingers, raspberries, whipped cream, and sherry pudding.

Lotus Blossom, looking very Irish in a green wool dress with a pretty lace collar, was somewhat taken aback when she saw the English trifle; she had brought all the ingredients for Irish coffee, including Jameson's Irish Whiskey.

Bertrand, resplendent in navy-blue doubled-breasted jacket, matching pants, and dapper ascot, was magnanimous. "We'll serve both. It will be our small effort toward building Irish-English relations."

Clancey stood close by Lotus Blossom's side. "Don't forget the Chinese," he added.

Sugar, in a pair of eye-catching orange toreador pants and top that should have clashed with her pink hair but somehow didn't, gaily clapped her hands. "Dinner's ready, everybody. Let's all sit down."

Amid much laughing and talking, the group was finally seated. Bobby offered grace.

Hearing the boy go through his list of thank yous to God, Gena could feel no remorse at having given his parents the money for his operation. If she hadn't, he wouldn't be alive with them today, so bright and happy and excited.

Gena peeked across the table at Peter. His head was bent, his hands clasped over his plate. In the time she had known him, she had never seen him look so young and relaxed. It even seemed he had gained some weight. Earlier today he had confided to Gena about a girl he liked. His face had glowed, talking about her. Gena gave thanks that a great burden had lifted from Peter's shoulders since his mother had started bringing home a regular paycheck. Now he had time to pursue interests that were normal for young men his age.

No, Gena decided, she could feel no remorse about any of those she had helped. How could she? She was only sorry for the way in which she had acquired the necessary money. Because her devious method of revenge was going to hurt Jarrod. But she had finally faced the fact that the longer she delayed her confession, the greater his hurt would be. Tonight, she had decided, she would tell him everything—and take the consequences.

Bobby's prayer ended, and the clatter of bowls and platters being passed, and plates being filled, began.

Bertrand rubbed his hands together in anticipation. "Thanksgiving is my favorite American holiday." He turned to Jarrod. "Somehow I've never been able to quite get into the spirit of the Fourth of July," he confided.

Jarrod raised his voice over the noise. "I've always wondered how a retired British actor ended up in Dallas."

" 'Ah, thereby hangs a tale!' Some years ago I came to the Colonies with a group of players. We undertook to tour the States. Alas, the group was somewhat second-rate. Our—I mean, their—reputation preceded us, and bookings were canceled. Thus I found myself stranded in Topeka." He turned to Bobby's mother, who was sitting on his left. "My dear, have you ever been to *Topeka*?" She shook her head, and he rolled his eyes heavenward. "Well, I checked my change pouch and found I only had funds to reach Cedar Rapids, Iowa, or Dallas, Texas."

"Why did you choose Dallas?" Bobby's mother asked.

"An excellent question. I have often asked it myself."

"I bet you wanted to see where J. R. Ewing lived, didn't you?" Bobby said, holding a full bowl of dressing in a death grip.

"My boy, I've never heard of the person. However, I must confess that I've enjoyed certain of John Wayne's films from time to time, and of course had heard much about the Alamo and Texas in general. All in all, Texas sounded infinitely more interesting; it triumphed hands down over Cedar Rapids."

"And we're all so glad it did," Sugar said, beaming at Bertrand. "He's such a talented man that we've long ago forgiven him."

"Bobby!" This time it was the little boy's father who spoke. "I think that's quite enough. If you eat everything you've managed to stuff on your plate, you'll be so full, we'll have to roll you out in a barrel."

Bertrand's white eyebrows waggled furiously up and down, and his voice boomed out across the table. "You've forgiven me! For what, madam?"

Sugar smiled benevolently. "Why, for being British, of course." To Bobby she said, "You see, we must really *thank* the British, because if they hadn't mistreated those poor Puritans so badly, we wouldn't be celebrating today."

"Actually they were exceedingly boring people, and we were more than delighted to see them leave."

Rose grinned. "I've always liked to think that there was at least one swinger among the bunch. After all, they were our forefathers, weren't they?"

Sugar ignored this and went on with Bobby's history lesson. "All the Puritans had with them when they arrived were the clothes on their backs. They had to grow their own food."

Bertrand swallowed a piece of turkey. "Had they not been such dull people, they would have ordered up a large hamper from Fortnum and Mason's."

"They weren't dull at all," Sugar corrected indignantly. "In fact they were quite *romantic* people. Captain John Smith fell in love with the beautiful Indian princess Pocahontas, and all because she taught him how to fish."

"You know that for a fact, do you, Sugar?" Jarrod asked, having a hard time repressing his laughter.

Gena reached beneath the table and took his hand.

Bobby's eyes had grown large. "Wow, Indians!"

"I've always wondered if 'making whoopee' was an Indian term," Rose said to no one in particular.

Sugar nodded at Jarrod's question and threw a bewildered glance at Rose before she went on.

"Pocahontas's father was going to have John Smith beheaded, but Pocahontas said—"

" 'No, no, a thousand times no!' " Bertrand intoned dramatically.

Sugar glared at him. "That's not what she said at all. She said, 'Don't touch a hair on this man's head. He's going to be your son-in-law.' "

Jarrod laughed, but Sugar seemed not to notice. "So they married and went back to England, where they met the queen and lived happily ever after."

Gena turned to Jarrod and caught him rubbing his temple with his forefinger, making tiny circles that clearly indicated "crazy." She choked back a laugh.

For Bobby's sake, if not her own, she felt compelled to straighten out Sugar's version of Thanksgiving. "That's not *quite* how it happened. For starters, John Smith was in Virginia—not Massachusetts."

Rose nodded. "And I'm sorry to tell you, Sugar, but Pocahontas saved John Smith's life quite a few years before the Pilgrims landed."

"It doesn't make any difference," Sugar maintained. "Theirs was a beautiful love story."

"Now, Sugar, I don't want you to be too disappointed," Gena said, "but Pocahontas and John Smith didn't even marry. Pocahontas married someone else."

"Ha! I don't believe that for a minute. Whyever would a sensible girl like that turn down a hunk like John Smith?"

Rose's ears pricked up. "A hunk? How do you know John Smith was a hunk?"

Sugar waved her fork in the air. "I'm certain he was. In fact I feel sure he looked much like Tyrone Power."

Bertrand looked down his long nose at Sugar. "I fear you have your films greatly confused, madam."

While stuffing food into his mouth, Bobby had been trying to follow the story. "But what about the Indians?"

"They taught the Pilgrims how to grow the food," Gena explained.

Rose fluttered her false eyelashes. "It must have been lots of fun—being taught by a group of well-built, half-naked savages."

Gena was determined to finish her explanation to Bobby. "To celebrate the first harvest, the Pilgrims invited the half-naked savages . . . er, I mean, the Indians to dinner."

Jarrod leaned over and whispered in her ear. "If the idea of a well-built, half-naked savage turns you on, I'll be glad to oblige tonight."

It didn't take long for Sugar and Bertrand to forget their disagreement, and the day was a great success. Jarrod, Gena, Rose, Peter, his sister, Bobby, and his dad played football later that afternoon. By the day's end everyone had eaten several more times and had sworn never to do so again.

That evening Gena sat at her dressing table. As she drew her brush through her hair with long, slow strokes, she could see Jarrod's reflection in her mirror. He was lying comfortably on her bed. Since the night the cookies-and-cream ice cream had melted on her night table, Jarrod had spent each night in her room.

In her head she began to phrase what she was about to say, but she heard him chuckle, and glanced into the mirror to see him smiling. "I would love to hear Sugar's version of the Christmas story."

"Sugar does have a tendency to view things in her own way." Gena flipped the long fall of her hair from one shoulder to the other, allowing it to shimmer over her breasts in an unbroken spill.

As she began to brush again, she suddenly realized that Jarrod would probably not be here for Christmas. Whether she would or not depended on the result of the conversation she now dreaded.

"Bobby has turned into quite a football player." In the mirror Jarrod grinned with satisfaction. "His dad actually thanked me for spending so many hours teaching Bobby to play football. It seems his dad has been doing a lot of overtime in order to get a promotion. The promotion finally came through, day before yesterday. Isn't that great?"

"It certainly is." Gena told herself she was prepared for any reaction Jarrod might have to her confession about the Sherwood Preservation Society. And she hoped she was right. However, her main concern was not for herself, but for Jarrod. If he decided to walk away once he'd heard what she had to say, she supposed she could face it. *As long as he walked away without pain!* She didn't think she could bear life without him *and* with the knowledge that she had hurt him badly. . . .

"Bobby's a great kid. I enjoyed every minute I spent with him. I'm almost sorry he doesn't need me anymore. Gena?" A pillow hit the back of her head. "Are you listening to me?"

She turned around. "Of course I am."

He laughed. "I don't think you are. All that turkey must have put you into a stupor."

She set down the brush. Her stomach was a tangle of nervous knots, but the time had come. She refused to put this off any longer. She took a deep breath. "Jarrod, I need to talk with you about something."

"Then come over here, because I need to talk to you about something too."

She reached for the light on her dressing table and switched it off, then rose and went to him. As she climbed onto the bed, he reached out to pull her down beside him.

"No, wait. There really is something I need to tell you."

She struggled to sit up, but he pressed her back into the bed. "Me first. I have something to tell you and I've really dreaded it."

Curious, she looked at him. "You've dreaded telling me something? What is it?"

"I have to fly back to Philadelphia tomorrow. A Saudi Arabian prince I've been courting is in the country. He wants to see me personally. His account could make a sizable difference in our balance sheet at the end of the year."

A fierce disappointment washed over Gena. Jarrod was leaving her! She had known this could happen at any time, of course, but now that it was an actuality, she felt vulnerable. "How long have you known?"

"Since yesterday. I didn't want to tell you until now, because I didn't want to spoil today."

She could understand that, she thought. She knew all about putting off bad news. "How long will you be gone?"

"Just a few days. I'll meet with the prince to-morrow afternoon, then take the weekend to con-fer with my people and put out a few fires I understand have gone out of control."

Gena couldn't fail to catch the excitement in his voice. "You miss the wheeling and dealing, don't you?"

"I'm not going to lie to you. I've missed it, but being here with you has been wonderful." Jarrod lowered his mouth to brush his lips across hers. "You and I have grown close in a way I never would have dreamed possible. As much pain as we've both experienced since your father's death, we've come out of it all with a love that runs deep and true."

Her hands traced the lines of his face, loving the feel of his weight on her. "You haven't men-tioned going back to stay permanently."

"I won't go without you."

"But you haven't asked me to go back either."

"When you're ready to leave here, you'll tell me. Until then I'm content to wait."

"Jarrod, you've changed so much."

"I've learned what's important. Teaching a child, doing odd jobs for a widow, laughing with friends, wearing jeans."

"Jeans?"

"Making slow, leisurely love to the only woman in the world I'll ever want."

Once more his lips claimed hers with a deepening kiss that drove all other things from her mind. No matter what happened between them in the future, Gena thought, she would have tonight.

Gena awoke. Her hand reached unerringly to the oposite side of the bed and found it vacant, and an incredible emptiness hit her as she realized that Jarrod had already gone.

She turned over and buried her face in the pillow. She could cope with the emptiness, she supposed. After all, he would only be gone a few days. But what she found harder to deal with was the pain of having let him go without telling him of her secret. Her opinion of herself in this regard fell even more markedly.

Yet, in thinking it through, Gena admitted that last night had not been the time to confess. Telling him she had embezzled his money—right before he was to leave for a trip—would not have been fair to either of them.

So she settled back to wait, preparing herself to tell Jarrod first thing when he returned Sunday night. And in the meantime she vowed to herself that she would not take one more cent from Alexander's.

Gena was kept busy in Jarrod's absence. Saturday night Clancey actually closed the bar early so that everyone could pitch in to put up Christmas decorations. This was unheard-of, but it had been Lotus Blossom's suggestion, and suddenly Clancey was wondering why he hadn't thought of Christmas decorations before.

Gena should have known what to expect of the decorations when a beaming Clancey told them of his "astute purchases" at a garage sale.

Nevertheless, nothing could have prepared her for the artifical tree that was so old that many of the needles dangled from plastic threads. Rose took one look at the tree and stated categorically that the rest of the needles would drop any minute, but Lotus Blossom declared it was the most beautiful tree she had ever seen, then discreetly took it out back and spray-painted it green.

Between the combined efforts of Jake, Peter, Gena, Rose, and Lotus Blossom the bar was eventually trimmed to Clancey's satisfaction.

A giant plastic Santa was a favorite of Clancey's, and he insisted that it stand right beside the tree. The Santa had a light bulb inside it, and when the figure was plugged in, one of its arms waved up and down. It glowed rather nicely. However, since the central stem of the artificial tree was bent, the tree leaned somewhat drunkenly against the Santa . . . whose arm kept going up and down with indefatigable good cheer. . . . They decided it didn't matter.

It took much spiked holiday cheer before the crew completed the decorating. The eggnog had been made according to a family recipe of Jake's. Rose kept "enhancing" it with profuse amounts of dark rum. By the time the revelers were halfway through their task, everyone was pleasantly high. No one understood why—but then, no one really cared. Gena laughed when Cole stuck his head in the door, saw Rose, and left again.

"If that man had a moustache, he'd twirl it," Rose muttered.

By the time they finished, all agreed that the bar had never looked better. Clancey had gotten a "deal" on tinsel, and they had strung it everywhere. Twinkling lights winked over the shelves where the liquor was stored, and gaudy Mexican poinsettias lurked in every corner. Rose had painted the nose on one of Clancey's deer heads a bright red, using nail polish. And finally, the group had tacked banded tinsel around the bar, which now looked as if it were wearing a silver hula skirt.

Gena glanced at her watch. "Hey, guys, I've got to get home. Jarrod said he would call me tonight."

"You go on ahead, honey," Rose said, tossing a handful of tinsel over Clancey's head to Peter. Half of it reached Peter—the other half rained on Clancey's balding head. "Tell Handsome to hurry back. I haven't found one tush worth pinching since he's been gone."

"I'll tell him."

Gena left the bar, humming softly. She was reeling pleasantly, but the walk home and the night air soon cleared her head. As she drew up in front of Sugar's, she saw a beige-colored Mercedes parked by the curb. She double-checked, but there was no way she could mistake the gleaming finish of the car. It belonged to Cole Garrett.

The slamming of the front door brought Gena's head around, and she watched Cole descend the steps.

"Gena, it's nice to see you alone, for a change! I was hoping to get a chance to talk to you earlier tonight, but I decided to wait."

"Oh?"

"It wasn't very smart of you to send Rose to my house the other night. You should have come yourself. It's true Rose is a very charming woman. Normally I would have been interested. But from the moment I saw you I haven't been able to think of anyone but you." As Gena absorbed the shock of his statement Cole added, "Now it's nearly too late."

"Nearly too late? What are you talking about?"

His hand closed over her long braid. "Go talk to Sugar. She'll probably be glad to see you. And perhaps"—his fingers fondled the braid—"perhaps we can work something out."

Gena pulled away. "Don't touch me, Cole, ever again!"

His mouth curved into an imitation of a smile. "We'll see. Before the week is out, you may be begging me to touch you. By the way, the more I think about it, the more I like that image. You begging me."

"Only in your fantasies, Cole."

"It won't be unpleasant, I assure you. But if you find the idea repugnant, just remember it's for Sugar. Good night."

Gena raced up the steps and into the house. At Sugar's door she knocked and waited. When there was no answer she knocked again. Cocking her head closer to the door, she heard the faint sounds of someone crying. She didn't wait. She turned the knob and entered.

Sugar was crumpled up on the sofa, sobbing her heart out. Gena went to her at once, and knelt beside her.

"Sugar, what on earth is wrong?"

Sugar raised her head, giving Gena a view of her tear-streaked face. Dark rivers of mascara had cut through the rouge and rice powder on her cheeks, and her candy-pink hair was in disarray. "Oh, Gena what am I going to do?"

Gena glanced around, looking for a box of tissues. When she found it, she pulled a handful from the box, and tenderly wiped Sugar's face clean. "Do about what?"

Sugar took the tissues from Gena's hand. "I didn't understand, or I never would have done it!" She paused to blow her nose loudly. "Tex would be so disappointed in me."

"Now, just calm down and tell me what exactly it is that you did. And what does Cole Garrett have to with it?"

Gena's questions set off a fresh torrent of tears from Sugar, and she decided stronger measures were called for. Fortunately she knew where Sugar kept her liquor supply, and she poured the older woman a hefty portion of whiskey.

"Take a deep breath, drink this, then tell me exactly what's happened."

Sugar gulped down several swallows. "Gena, it's just terrible!"

"I don't care how bad it is. I want you to tell me."

"Okay. Five years ago"—Sugar hiccupped—"I found out that most of the money Tex left me was gone. I don't know where it went to, you understand. Goodness knows I never spent much." She hiccupped again. "Just a pair of toreador pants here and there, but the upkeep on this house was just too much, I suppose."

Gena nodded understandingly.

"Well, I realized that I couldn't pay the mortgage on the house anymore. But I couldn't bring myself to sell the place where Tex and I had been so happy. So I had the idea of turning some of the rooms into apartments." Her face fell. "The only problem was, I didn't have the money to do that either. Then I met Cole Garrett."

"Did he loan you the money?"

Sugar nodded. "Twenty thousand dollars, just the sum I needed to complete the renovations. He even said he would pay my property taxes for the next five years. He said he was doing it for his own tax write-off. It sounded like a wonderful deal."

"But the five years are up and you don't have the money to repay him? Is that it?"

"Oh, I've saved, really I have. I now have nearly twenty thousand dollars. Well . . . almost."

"Good!" Gena patted her arm. "Then there's no problem."

"That's what I thought, too, until Cole told me differently." Sugar took another drink of whiskey. "You see, I had to use my house as collateral."

"I figured that. But if you pay him back, your house will be safe, right?"

"Not exactly." Sugar emptied the glass and handed it to Gena. "May I have some more?"

"No! Now tell me what *exactly* were the conditions of the loan?"

"Cole had me sign a statement that stipulated he was loaning me twenty thousand dollars. That was the value of the house at the time." She stopped and grabbed a piece of paper off the coffee table. "Oh, here, you read it! I just can't understand. Cole can't be right. He says I owe him a hundred and fifty thousand dollars!"

For the first time in her life Gena felt close to fainting. "*What?*" She took the document and quickly scanned it. "Dear Lord, Sugar, you signed something stating that at the end of five years, you'd owe Cole the current market value of your house. That creep! That first class bastard! As a real-estate developer, he knew that the real-estate market was changing in this area. Prices were bound to go way up. In the past few years, houses in this neighborhood have been restored right and left. . . ."

Sugar was close to tears again. "So is he right? Do I owe him that much money?" She got up to help herself to more whiskey. She didn't bother to pour it into a glass. She brought the bottle back with her.

Gena didn't stop her. In fact she felt like joining her, but she knew that someone had to keep a clear head. "I'm afraid so. We can have our own appraisal made, of course, but I'm pretty sure the amount Cole quoted isn't too far off the mark. For all his bad qualities, and he has many, he's a shrewd man when it comes to business. Why on earth didn't you tell me before now? We could have been working this out together."

"I know, but I was just so sure everything would be okay."

Gena sighed. "What's your deadline, Sugar? How long do you have to come up with the money?"

"Until next Thursday. That's five days away."

"And how much have you saved exactly?"

"Eleven thousand, four hundred and fifty dollars."

"I thought you said you had most of the twenty thousand saved!"

"That *is* most of it, isn't it? I thought I had done real well. But things happen. You know, like when the plumbing burst and we had to call in that nice young plumber. Remember?"

"I remember. I think he charged you for three extra visits just so he could come back to see Rose."

"No, I'm sure he wouldn't have charged me without reason." She took a swig from the bottle. "He was too nice."

Gena took the bottle from Sugar's hands and set it aside. "Sugar, you must develop a more realistic view of the world! Things are not as romantic as you would like. Plumbers do overcharge, and unscrupulous people will try to take advantage of you. You've got to toughen up. Romantics have a hard time in life—reality can be very harsh!"

Sugar let her head drop to the back of the sofa and sighed sadly. "I've always thought our lives would be so much prettier if they were scored musically. You know, like movies. Any scene, even an ugly one, takes on more beauty when music is played."

Gena groaned, but her heart went out to her friend. For the first time since she had known her, Sugar actually looked old. "Sugar, this isn't the movies."

"No, but wouldn't it be nice if it were?"

"Yes," Gena said gently, pulling Sugar's legs up onto the couch and covering her with an afghan. "Yes, it would. Now, just go to sleep and don't worry anymore. I'll take care of it."

"Thank you. I believe I will sleep," the older woman murmured. Her eyes drifted closed.

Gena let herself quietly out of the room, then hurried up to her apartment. Jarrod would call tonight, but even better, he would be back tomorrow. She knew that once he heard Sugar's story, he would agree that they had to give her the money.

The phone was ringing as she let herself in. She managed to pick it up on the fourth ring. "Hello?"

"Gena, I'm so glad I caught you. Half a minute more, and I would have had to give up."

She sank onto the bed. "Jarrod, it's great to hear your voice. I wish you were here."

"I wish I were, too, babe. But I'm afraid I've got some bad news."

"Oh, no!"

"I won't be home tomorrow night as planned. I'm at the airport right now. They've already given the final boarding call for my plane, so just listen. Something has come up, and I must fly back to Saudi Arabia with the prince. It's absolutely essential."

"But Jarrod—"

"I know, honey, but I'll be home in a week. We'll talk then. I love you, don't ever forget how much. Gotta go. 'Bye."

Slowly Gena hung up the phone, her eyes fixed unseeingly on the distant wall. What was she going to do now?

Nine

The next day was Sunday. Sugar's distress was obvious to her friends, and soon Bertrand and Rose had been advised of her problem. Rose was ready to put out a contract on Cole. Bertrand declared Cole to be a bounder of the first order and suggested that the authorities be called in, but Gena advised him that what Cole was doing was perfectly legal, no matter how morally wrong.

While Bertrand and Rose fumed, Gena spent all day turning the problem around in her head, examining it from every angle. And despite the agonizing hours spent, she always returned to the same conclusion. It was true she had vowed never again to take money from Alexander's, but it was also true that there was no way she could sit idly by and let Sugar lose her house.

Jarrod would understand, she told herself. He would have to. But as the night wore on, the doubts and uncertainties lingered, and sleep eluded her until dawn.

A few short hours later Gena was awake. She took the briefcase from under her bed, plugged it in, keyed in the necessary commands to complete the sign-on process, then completed and verified the transaction.

She sat back amazed. How could such a simple, easy procedure that didn't take a great deal of time solve Sugar's problem and at the same time worsen Gena's?

Wednesday evening, high in the air somewhere between Philadelphia and Dallas, Jarrod handed his empty cup back to the flight attendant. Fortunately he didn't feel that tired. He had been able to finish his business in Saudi Arabia and catch a return plane to the States within hours. He had slept all the way back to Philadelphia, where he had stopped over only long enough to change clothes and pick up some paper work his assistant had prepared for him.

Glancing out the window, he saw that the sun was sinking lower in the sky. He knew it would be dark by the time he landed and drove to the boarding house.

Automatically he opened a file, but he didn't start to read immediately. Instead he thought of Gena. He couldn't wait to see her again. Granted they had been apart only days, but it had been enough to convince him that he never again wanted to be parted from her. From now on if he had to go away on business, she would come with him.

He smiled at his own presumption. So much for tolerance and patience. But their newfound closeness was such a precious thing to him, he could stand no more indecision about their future. Tonight they would discuss the rest of their lives.

Reluctantly he turned his attention to the file before him on the pull-down tray. His assistant had told him a group of auditors they had hired had found something that warranted an explanation from him.

It seemed that, following routine procedure, the auditors had selected a file at random. When they traced its history, the supporting documentation for the file could not be found. And when they dug further and found less, they were puzzled. Since the creation records showed that Jarrod had initiated this account, they were requesting an explanation from him so they could complete the audit.

What the hell was going on? he thought. He had never created a file for a charity called . . . the Sherwood Preservation Society. *What?*

They had given him an extraction of the audit file that traced the Sherwood's account history. His eyes scanned the extraction until they came across a familiar word . . . *Gena. Gena?* Incredulously he looked at it, disbelieving. But there it was. One word. *Gena.*

What did it mean? With a sinking heart he reviewed the file once more—and then he knew. Beyond a doubt. She had left her name for him as a clue, knowing that if the Sherwood account were called up on an audit, he would know this had been her doing.

Damn! He leaned back against the headrest and closed his eyes. *Damn!*

His mind went ten different directions at once. Gena had been systematically taking money from the company he was in control of, using his name. The reason why wasn't a puzzle. Running away from him hadn't been enough for her. She had gone one step further in venting her anger. Because she felt he had betrayed her, she in turn had betrayed him.

And if it hadn't been for this random audit, he might never have known. Had she thought of telling him? he wondered.

He would have sworn that over the past few weeks their love had grown to the point that any lingering anger she might have felt toward him had disappeared. But she hadn't told him! That hurt. It hurt so much.

Then he remembered that the night before he left, she'd said there was something she must discuss with him. Had she planned to tell him then?

He opened his eyes and looked back down at the print-out. Before him were dates, amounts, and transactions, all in neat black figures, in neat even rows. There were quite a few. He looked at the dates. Two had been made since he had found her—one shortly after he arrived in Dallas, and one . . . one since he had been in Saudi Arabia. And the amount was one hundred and fifty thousand dollars!

Suddenly a cold fear climbed up his spine. Lord in heaven, could she possibly have taken the money and run away again?

No! He wouldn't let himself even think it. He was going to trust her. There was an explanation for all of this. It might not be a *reasonable* explanation, but he didn't care, because he understood. Like his jealousy, emotions involving love were seldom clear or logical or reasonable.

She would tell him, he was sure of it. In the meantime he had to figure out how to clear her with the auditors. As of now, no one but he suspected anything underhanded. All the auditors wanted was the supporting documentation.

He would have to work like hell to invent an incident explaining how the supporting documentation had been lost. But he would find something! Something they would believe. There really would be no reason for the auditors to mistrust him. Gena's secret would be safe.

When the certified check arrived from the Sherwood Preservation Society, there was much rejoicing among the residents of the house. Bertrand went out and bought a half dozen bottles of champagne. Rose cooked up her version of West Texas chili, containing absolutely no venison, but as hot as Hades.

When Jarrod let himself in the front door of the house, he heard the music and laughter issuing from Sugar's apartment. Since the door was open he walked in, then came to a standstill just inside the sitting room.

Gena and Bertrand were doing a stately waltz around the room, completely out of time with "Let's Spend the Night Together," the Rolling Stones song that blared forth from Sugar's old radio.

Clancey and Lotus Blossom cuddled on the couch, oblivious to anyone else in the room.

From his vantage point, Jarrod could also see through an arched doorway into the dining room, where Rose was poised on the dining-room table. In her stockinged feet she was doing the limbo dance beneath the light fixture, a champagne glass balanced on her forehead.

Sugar was nowhere to be seen.

With Gena in his arms, Bertrand executed a perfect twirl, then descended to a dip. Gena's long blond hair flowed down to the faded, flower-patterned carpet.

She wore the amber silk dress he had bought for her, and Jarrod thought she had never looked more beautiful. He forgot his hurt when he'd first discovered she had taken money from his company. He forgot everything but how relieved he was that she was still here, and how he wanted her with an unmistakable urgency. . . .

Still balanced over Bertrand's arm as she dipped, Gena turned her head slightly and saw him. "Jarrod!" The moment Bertrand lifted her to a standing position, she broke out of his hold and ran into Jarrod's arms. "I'm so glad to see you, but I thought you wouldn't be back until the end of the week!"

"It didn't take as long as I'd thought."

"Great! You're just in time for a celebration."

"Hiya, Handsome," Rose called from the table-top. "Grab a glass of champagne and join me. Dining-room tables offer lots of possibilities. We could explore them all."

"I'm afraid I'd break Sugar's table. You come down."

Rose's cheeks dimpled with delight. "I'll be right there."

"So what are you celebrating, anyway?" he asked.

"Lotus Blossom and Clancey are engaged," Gena told him.

"Wonderful!" Jarrod turned to the happy couple, still welded together on the sofa. "Congratulations!"

Clancey's face wrinkled into a grin.

"Thanks, Jarrod," Lotus Blossom said sweetly.

"Have you set the date?"

"Not yet, but we're hoping it will be soon."

"And we have more to celebrate," Rose said, coming up to Jarrod and planting a big kiss on his cheek. "Bertrand, tell him your news."

"I have been given a contract to do a series of

commercials for an excellent haberdashery here in town."

"Bertrand finally thinks he's found something suitably dignified."

"Actually there's nothing dignified in hawking someone else's dry goods," the retired actor corrected, "but it is the lesser of many evils."

"Such as starvation?" Rose kidded.

"Precisely, my dear. And such as pandering to a feline with bladder problems."

Sugar came through the door from the kitchen. "Jarrod, it's perfect that you're back! Now our little group is complete."

"Tell him of your good fortune, madam," Bertrand directed.

Beside him Jarrod felt Gena stiffen, and shot her a curious glance before he turned his attention to Sugar.

"Oh, you'll just never believe it, Jarrod. I was about to lose my beloved home—"

"To that reptile Cole Garrett," Rose muttered.

"And a miracle occurred."

"Miracle?" Jarrod asked. Bobby had used the same word, describing how his mother had received a check for his heart operation. Suddenly pieces began falling into place for him.

"I owed him a hundred and fifty thousand dollars! Well, today, one day before my deadline, I received a certified check for the exact amount needed to pay off Cole. I'd saved some money, too, and that's my nest egg. So now no one will ever be able to take my house away from me! Tex would have been so happy." Sugar's eyes misted. "I wish he were here, but I shouldn't complain. I have all of you."

Rose put an arm over Sugar's shoulder and hugged her. "You sure do, sweetie. And if you ever have a problem, all you got to do is call."

Sugar patted Rose's hand. "Thank you. Now, Jarrod, you must have some of Rose's chili."

"It's guaranteed to grow hair between your toes," Rose said cheerfully.

"No, thank you, I—"

"I'm going back to the bar to get us some beer," Clancey announced, lurching up from the couch.

Lotus Blossom jumped up after him. "You can't, Clancey. You've had too much to drink."

"I'm tired of champagne. I want some Lone Star," he insisted. "I'll be fine."

"No you won't," the bride-to-be said firmly. "I'll drive."

"I tell you what," Jarrod said. "Gena and I will drive over and get the beer. I'd like a chance to say hello to her in private."

Rose clapped her hands together. "Nice idea, Handsome! Are there more at home like you?"

"I'm afraid not."

"Pity."

"Gena?"

She smiled. "I agree with Rose. It's a wonderful idea. Clancey, give me your keys. We'll be right back with your beer."

Lotus Blossom took the keys out of Clancey's hand and tossed them to Jarrod. "Thank you. I'd hate for him to die before I can get him to the altar."

Clancey folded his hands across his chest and grinned like a bronzed Buddha.

Gena sat close to Jarrod in the car, her happiness at seeing him overriding everything else. Once inside Clancey's, she fell into his arms and hugged him to her. She felt so warm and secure there and Jarrod seemed to need the contact as much as she.

His arms were tightly around her, his face buried in her hair. The bar was dark except for the dim light on in the hallway and a few of the neon beer signs that were lit. It was lovely just to hold and to be held in the quiet emptiness of the place. But after a moment Gena pulled away. There would be no more delays.

"Jarrod, I've got to tell you something about the money that Sugar received."

"Later, later," he murmured, his blood stirred. He had never wanted her more than at this moment.

His hand slipped under the full skirt of the dress. She was wearing only panties, and his fingers found their way inside to the waiting warmth of her and moved until she was quivering with need.

"How do you know just where to touch me?" she whispered, leaning weakly against him, her mouth brushing over the skin of his throat as she talked.

"Because I love you."

Quickly he peeled off her panties, then lifted her and placed her on a barstool. Instinctively her legs wrapped around his waist. He unbuttoned the shirtwaist bodice of the dress. She unhooked the waistband of his pants. He pushed the top of the dress off her shoulders and her waist. She unzipped his fly, then reached for him.

Jarrod groaned. "And how do you know exactly how to touch me?"

"Because I love you."

"That was the right answer," he muttered hoarsely before grinding his mouth against hers.

Gena pulled away from him.

"What will my right answer get me?" she murmured.

"What do you want?"

With her hands still on him, she gently guided him into her, then gasped as she felt his fullness inside. "This, only this."

His hips began to move and she held him tightly: within, without.

"I think I'm going to buy Clancey a pool table," Jarrod said.

Gena lay stretched out beside him on the bar, her head cradled in the crook of his shoulder. She supposed they must look silly lying here, but she didn't care.

"A pool table sounds promising."

"And wider. I never realized how narrow a bar could be."

"That's because it wasn't built for this."

"You didn't say for *making love*."

"For making love," she repeated dutifully.

"I wonder if there's a repeated market for wider bars that's being overlooked?"

"Always the businessman."

"No, always the lover."

"I approve."

"Gena?"

"Yes?"

"I don't want to alarm you, but there seems to be someone over there by the Christmas tree."

"*What?* Oh. That's Clancey's Santa. He waves and glows."

"Waves and glows. I think I was away too long." He dropped a kiss on her temple. "Do you think we'd better get Clancey his beer?" he asked.

"Clancey can wait. Jarrod?"

"Umm?"

"I love you."

"And I love you."

"I've been embezzling your money." Well, there it was, Gena thought. Out in the open at last. For a moment all was silent, except for the thunderous pounding of her heart.

"I know."

"I don't think you understand what I just said. When I moved here, I was furious with you, and almost simultaneously I discovered people who desperately needed help."

"I know, Gena."

"But how?"

"An accounting firm was retained to prepare Alexander's for a potential audit. They selected the Sherwood Preservation Society as a random sample. Irregularities were discovered. I was given the Sherwood file so that I could explain these."

She brought her hands up to hide her face. "Oh, Jarrod, I'm so sorry. I wanted to tell you myself. I meant to. I tried to!"

He pulled her hands back down and held them. "I know. I stopped you Thanksgiving night. I'm sorry."

"No! Don't apologize." She pulled herself onto one elbow and looked down at him. "When I heard about your father, I wanted to die. I was so afraid you'd feel that you, too, had been betrayed and would be hurt!"

Tenderly Jarrod cupped her cheek. "Hey! There's *no* comparison here! In fact it never even entered my mind."

"Thank goodness for that. But I want to explain to you, so you'll understand."

"I think I do. You were angry at me."

"Yes, but it was more than that. I didn't take the money for myself. For the first time in my life I found myself surrounded by needy people, and I was frustrated that I couldn't help them."

"Bobby was one of those people, wasn't he?"

"Yes. Jarrod, if you could have seen that child before his operation, you wouldn't have recognized him as the happy little boy he is today. He was pale and thin, unable to play. I couldn't let him die. So I thought of a way to help him."

"You could have contacted me. I would have given you the money. Gena, there's something you must understand. I've never considered Alexander's mine. I've run it for you, but I've never drawn a penny in salary for doing it."

In the darkness Gena wiped a tear from her eye. "I couldn't have contacted you then. I was too angry and confused; I had too much to work through. But Jarrod, I'm so glad you found me."

"There was never any question that I would. We were meant to be together."

She leaned to place a kiss on his lips. "Do you forgive me?"

"If you'll forgive me."

"For what?"

"For being so driven, for not sitting you down immediately following the reading of the will and making you understand, for not being as perfect a person as you deserve."

"Stop it!" She covered his mouth with hers in a soul-felt kiss. "The past is behind us," she murmured when she'd raised her head. "Our future is beginning right now."

"Right now," Jarrod agreed, and pulled her back to him.

When they arrived at Sugar's they fully expected everyone to be asleep. But they found Sugar's door open, and peeked in.

Rose, Sugar, Bertrand, Clancey, and Lotus Blossom sat silently around the room. Clancey was holding an ice pack to his head. Sugar was struggling to open the safety cap on an aspirin bottle. Bertrand appeared to have fallen asleep sitting up. Rose was building a pyramid out of empty champagne glasses. And Lotus Blossom was staring at nothing in particular.

"Hi, everybody. Is the party over?"

Bertrand opened one eye. "We're not entirely certain."

Arm in arm Gena and Jarrod entered the room.

"What's going on?" she asked. "Are you waiting for the beer? We've got it out in the car."

Clancey took the ice pack from his head. "Gena, could you talk a little more softly please?"

"Is someone going to tell us what's going on?"

Suddenly Sugar brought the aspirin bottle down on the table with a tremendous thud. Clancey groaned. The bottle broke open, and aspirin flew everywhere. Sugar scrambled to pick up two.

Rose waved a hand toward the champagne-glass pyramid. "We finished all the champagne."

"And then we started on my liquor cabinet," Sugar said.

Lotus Blossom spoke up. "We not only started, we finished, her liquor cabinet."

"We should have come back sooner," Jarrod murmured to Gena.

Rose rubbed her forehead and eyed the pyramid critically. "Oh, you haven't heard the best part."

"Well, I'm glad to hear there is a good part,"

Gena said, hands on her hips. She felt as if she were facing a schoolroom full of naughty children.

Sugar swallowed the two aspirin, then reached for another. "You'll like this part. We decided that we should get even with Cole Garrett, so we piled into Rose's car and went to his house."

"I'm not sure I want to hear this," Jarrod muttered. "Our companies employ a whole team of lawyers, but I doubt even they could handle something of this magnitude."

"His car was sitting out front, and Rose broke into it."

Jarrod looked at Rose. "How did you do that?"

"I've got all kinds of talents, honey."

"Anyway," Sugar said, "Bertrand got the garden hose, and we filled that sucker up with water."

Clancey, deciding to join the conversation, nodded sagely. "Water."

Gena couldn't believe what she was hearing. "You filled Cole's Mercedes with water?"

"As near to the top as we could."

Rose placed another glass atop the pyramid. "And then we slipped a catfish through an opening we'd left at the top of the window."

Clancey smiled hugely. "Catfish."

"That was the *meanest*, *biggest* catfish I've ever seen," Sugar exclaimed.

"Where in the world did you get a catfish?" Jarrod asked.

"We've been unable to answer that particular question," Bertrand answered glumly.

Gena grabbed Jarrod's arm for support. "What?"

Sugar shrugged. "We haven't a clue."

"I say, old chap, we need a camera. You wouldn't happen to know where we could get one, do you?"

"What do you need a camera for?" Jarrod asked.

"We want to be there in the morning when that snake Cole sees his car," Rose explained. "Then Sugar is going to hand him the check. That should wilt his designer suit."

All of a sudden the champagne-glass pyramid came crashing down. Everyone ducked.

"Okay, all to bed!" Gena ordered. "In the morning Jarrod will take the check to Cole, giving him time, of course, to get over the shock of his car."

"Why don't we have the check messengered," Jarrod suggested. "I'm not sure I could keep a straight face."

"We want to make sure he doesn't mistreat the catfish," Sugar said.

"I wish I could remember where we got the thing," Bertrand said, taking great care to keep his head level as he rose.

"Go to bed, everyone. Now!" Gena smiled. "Tomorrow Jarrod and I have some things to tell you."

"Great," Rose said. "You're finally going to tell us that you and Jarrod are rich and that you're responsible for the 'miracles' that have been happening since you came to live here."

Gena nodded weakly. "Uh, right."

"Okay, then, we'll see you as soon as we're able to function. Since I have no idea when that might be, don't call us, we'll call you. Come on, Bertrand, I'll race you up the stairs."

"Surely you jest!"

"Me, jest?" Rose winked at Gena and Jarrod as she took Bertrand's arm and led him out the door. "I love making men wonder."

Sugar wandered off in the direction of her bedroom, leaving Gena and Jarrod alone with Clancey and Lotus Blossom, who had fallen asleep on the couch, their arms entwined.

Jarrod looked at Gena and put his fingers to his lips. "Come on, let's go upstairs so we don't wake them up."

"Wake them up!" she whispered. "Are you kidding? They'll all be out until this time tomorrow."

A few minutes later Gena was snuggled next to Jarrod in her bed.

"How do you suppose Rose knew about you?" Jarrod asked.

"She's a smart lady. Beneath her flakey exterior there's a lot that would surprise you."

"She's wonderful, isn't she? They all are. Will you hate leaving here very much?"

"Yes. And no. I'm ready to go back with you, but I do hate leaving them here alone." She giggled. "Good heavens, we were gone only a little while tonight, and look what they got into!"

"They'll be okay. We'll keep an eye on them. I'd like to keep on renting this room. Just so we can come back every so often."

"Really?" Gena was touched at this evidence

that Jarrod had come to love the residents of the boarding house as much as she did.

"Yeah. I love the idea of bringing our babies to see Auntie Sugar and Auntie Rose."

It didn't even occur to her to question Jarrod's casual reference to babies, so natural did it seem. "Don't forget Auntie Lotus Blossom."

Jarrod chuckled. "Or Uncle Bertrand and Uncle Clancey."

"Good heavens, no! Jarrod?" Hesitantly she smiled up at him. "I want to expand the operations of the Sherwood Preservation Society and carry on with it. I figure a charity can operate out of Philadelphia as well as Dallas."

"If you hadn't suggested it, I would have." He kissed her softly. "I love you, babe."

"I love you too."

"Gena?"

"Ummm?"

"Where do you suppose they got that catfish?"

THE EDITOR'S CORNER

We have Valentine's Day presents galore for you next month . . . hearts, flowers, chuckles, and a sentimental tear or two. We haven't wrapped your presents in the traditional colors of the special holiday for lovers, though. Rather, we're presenting them in a spectrum of wonderful earth colors from vibrant, exhilarating Green to sinfully rich chocolate Brown. (Apologies to Billie and Sandra for using their last names this way, but I couldn't resist!)

First, in **MAKIN' WHOOPEE,** LOVESWEPT #182, by—of course—Billie Green, you'll discover the perfect Valentine's Day heroine, Sara Love. Ms. Love's business partner (and sweet nemesis) is the wickedly good-looking Charlie Sanderson. These two charmers have been waging a long silent battle to repress their true feelings for one another. He has built for himself a reputation as "Good Time Charlie," the swinging bachelor; she has built walls around her emotions, pouring all her energies into the business. An ill-fated trip to inspect a piece of property is the catalyst for the erosion of their defenses, but it isn't until a little bundle of joy makes an astonishing appearance that these two humorous and heartwarming and sexy people come together at last . . . and forever. With all the freshness, optimism, and excitement we associate with the green of springtime, Billie creates in **MAKIN' WHOOPEE** two characters whose love story you'll long remember.

TANGLES, LOVESWEPT #183, by Barbara Boswell, is a story that dazzled me so much I see it as painted in brilliant yellows and golds. Barbara's heroine, Krista Conway, is a highpowered divorce lawyer who is as beautiful as she is brainy. And to hero Logan Moore, the new judge who is trying Krista's case, she is the most seductive lady he's ever laid eyes on. Now Krista may appear hard as nails, but beneath her beautiful and sophisticated exterior is a

(continued)

tender woman who yearns for a man to love and a family to care for. Logan is one heck of a sexy widower with three delightful children . . . and he's a man who is badly misled by Krista's image and wildly confused by his compelling need for her. In a series of events that by turns sizzle with love and romance and sear with emotional intensity, the **TANGLES** these two wonderful people find themselves in begin to unravel to an unexpectedly beautiful ending. Bravo, Barbara Boswell!

The warm earth colors of orange, pale to dusky, had to have been on the palette of Anne and Ed Kolaczyk as they created **SULTRY NIGHTS,** LOVE-SWEPT #184. In this poignant romance of love lost and love regained, we encounter Rachel Anders years after her passionate affair with Ben Healey. One brilliant, erotic, tenderly emotional summer was all Rachel and Ben had together before he had to leave town. Rachel lived on in pained loss, faced with Ben's silence, and comforted only by the legacy of their passion, a beloved daughter. When they meet again, the attraction between them is fired to even greater heat than they'd known in their youth. But Rachel's secret still will come between them until they find their own path to a love that time could not destroy. Ablaze with intensity, **SULTRY NIGHTS** is a captivating love story.

Sandra Brown is a remarkably talented and hardworking author who seems phenomenal to me in the way she keeps topping herself in the creation of one wonderful love story after another. And here comes another of her delectably sensual love stories, **SUNNY CHANDLER'S RETURN,** LOVESWEPT #185. I referred above to "sinfully rich chocolate." I must have written those words because unconsciously I was still under the sway of a very short, but never-to-be forgotten episode in this book involving triple dipped strawberries. (See if you don't delight in that scene as much as I did.) And speaking of people who are

(*continued*)

phenomenal in topping themselves, I must mention Barbara Alpert who writes all the splendid back cover copy for our LOVESWEPTs. Her description of Sandra's next book is so terrific that I'm going to give you a sneak preview of the back cover copy. Here's what Barbara wrote.

"The whispers began when she entered the ballroom—and every male eye in the place was caught by the breathtakingly lovely spitfire with the slightly shady reputation. Ty Beaumont knew a heartbreaker when he saw one—and also knew that nothing and nobody could keep him from making her his inside a week's time. He'd bet a case of Wild Turkey on it! Sunny heard his devil's voice drawl in her ear, and couldn't help but notice the man was far too handsome for his own good, but his fierce ardor sparked hers, and his "I'll have you naked yet" smile caused a kind of spontaneous combustion that nothing could quench. Private torments had sent both Ty and Sunny racing from the past, but would revealing their dark secrets let them face the future together?"

We think next month offers you a particularly exciting quartet of LOVESWEPTs, and we hope you enjoy each one immensely.

With every good wish,

Carolyn Nichols

Carolyn Nichols
 Editor
LOVESWEPT
Bantam Books, Inc.
666 Fifth Avenue
New York, NY 10103

Heirs to a great dynasty, the Delaney brothers were united by blood, united by devotion to their rugged land . . . and known far and wide as

---

THE SHAMROCK TRINITY

Bantam's bestselling LOVESWEPT romance line built its reputation on quality and innovation. Now, a remarkable and unique event in romance publishing comes from the same source: THE SHAMROCK TRINITY, three daringly original novels written by three of the most successful women's romance writers today. Kay Hooper, Iris Johansen, and Fayrene Preston have created a trio of books that are dynamite love stories bursting with strong, fascinating male and female characters, deeply sensual love scenes, the humor for which LOVESWEPT is famous, and a deliciously fresh approach to romance writing.

THE SHAMROCK TRINITY—Burke, York, and Rafe: Powerful men . . . rakes and charmers . . . they needed only love to make their lives complete.

☐ *RAFE, THE MAVERICK by Kay Hooper*

Rafe Delaney was a heartbreaker whose ebony eyes held laughing devils and whose lilting voice could charm any lady—or any horse—until a stallion named Diablo left him in the dust. It took Maggie O'Riley to work her magic on the impossible horse . . . and on his bold owner. Maggie's grace and strength made Rafe yearn to share the raw beauty of his land with her, to teach her the exquisite pleasure of yielding to the heat inside her. Maggie was stirred by Rafe's passion, but would his reputation and her ambition keep their kindred spirits apart?   (21786 • $2.50)

LOVESWEPT

☐ *YORK, THE RENEGADE by Iris Johansen*

Some men were made to fight dragons, Sierra Smith thought when she first met York Delaney. The rebel brother had roamed the world for years before calling the rough mining town of Hell's Bluff home. Now, the spirited young woman who'd penetrated this renegade's paradise had awakened a savage and tender possessiveness in York: something he never expected to find in himself. Sierra had known loneliness and isolation too—enough . to realize that York's restlessness had only to do with finding a place to belong. Could she convince him that love was such a place, that the refuge he'd always sought was in her arms?

(21787 • $2.50)

☐ *BURKE, THE KINGPIN by Fayrene Preston*

Cara Winston appeared as a fantasy, racing on horseback to catch the day's last light—her silver hair glistening, her dress the color of the Arizona sunset . . . and Burke Delaney wanted her. She was on his horse, on his land: she would have to belong to him too. But Cara was quicksilver, impossible to hold, a wild creature whose scent was midnight flowers and sweet grass. Burke had always taken what he wanted, by willing it or fighting for it; Cara cherished her freedom and refused to believe his love would last. Could he make her see he'd captured her to have and hold forever?

(21788 • $2.50)